"We've said all there is to say about the money. I do understand."

"Then you're an extraordinarily understanding woman." Russ wanted to take her in his arms and kiss her until they were both out of breath, kiss her until she agreed not to hurry back to New York. But he didn't like his chances. So he settled for a long hug.

"I'm glad I met you, Sydney Baines."

"I'm not gone yet."

Yeah, but she would be going soon. They always left eventually. He'd always recovered and moved on. But every time he looked at her he felt an ache in his chest.

And he knew that she was going to be harder to get over than all the rest....

Dear Reader,

Did you know that you might have money stashed away somewhere you don't even know about? Forgotten bank accounts, utility deposits and other property have been abandoned all over the United States. There are private investigators who devote their lives to reuniting people with their unclaimed property.

When I first read about this many years ago, it sparked my imagination. So I created Sydney, an "heir-finder" P.I., and Russ, a man whose principles are so strong he refuses to accept an inheritance from the father who abandoned him. The clash of wills that follows was a lot of fun to write, and though the story was rejected multiple times over the years, I loved it so much I kept revising until I got it right.

I hope you enjoy Sydney and Russ's story and the Texas Hill Country setting—also very special to me. Then find out if *you* have unclaimed funds by checking on the Web. (I recently discovered $141.00 owed to my husband.)

Sincerely,

*Kara Lennox*

# ONE STUBBORN TEXAN
## Kara Lennox

HARLEQUIN®

TORONTO • NEW YORK • LONDON
AMSTERDAM • PARIS • SYDNEY • HAMBURG
STOCKHOLM • ATHENS • TOKYO • MILAN • MADRID
PRAGUE • WARSAW • BUDAPEST • AUCKLAND

ISBN-13: 978-0-373-75184-6
ISBN-10:    0-373-75184-2

ONE STUBBORN TEXAN

## ABOUT THE AUTHOR

Texas native Kara Lennox has earned her living at various times as an art director, typesetter, textbook editor and reporter. She's worked in a boutique, a health club and an ad agency. She's been an antiques dealer and even a blackjack dealer. But no work has made her happier than writing romance novels. She has written more than fifty books.

When not writing, Kara indulges in an ever-changing array of hobbies. Her latest passions are bird-watching and long-distance bicycling. She loves to hear from readers; you can visit her Web page at www.karalennox.com.

## Books by Kara Lennox

### HARLEQUIN AMERICAN ROMANCE

*Blond Justice
**Firehouse 59

# Chapter One

"Stranger's coming," Bert Klausen announced from his perch by the front window of the Linhart General Store. Bert, former owner of the store and now firmly retired, spent most of his winter days in a rocking chair warming himself by the wood-burning stove, staring out the window and munching on dill pickles. No one came or went in Linhart, Texas, without Bert's knowing.

Russ Klein added an extra scoop of coffee grounds to the pot he was making. Maybe it was a customer.

"It's a female, and quite a looker, too. She drives a beemer," Bert announced between crunches on his pickle. "A white one."

"BMW, huh?" Russ ambled to the front of the store, pretending to straighten the camping gear as he went. He stepped over Nero, the bloodhound asleep on the floor, and opened the stove to poke at the burning logs with a stick. That time waster complete, he closed the grate and peered out the window; a cold drizzle made everything outside look gray and depressing. He couldn't miss the snazzy white car parked across the street, but the driver was nowhere to be seen.

"Went inside the post office," Bert said, answering Russ's unasked question.

"Mmm-hmm."

"Maybe she'll come in here when she gets done there," Bert mused hopefully. The wilderness outfitting business wasn't exactly brisk this time of year, not like spring and summer, when tourists and college kids streamed in by the dozens to stock up on food, beer and camping supplies. Breaks in the winter monotony were scarce.

"Maybe," Russ agreed with practiced indifference, though his gaze never left the white car. He wondered what other excuse he could find to linger at the front of the store. A stranger in town on a cold, gray weekday was cause for curiosity. A female stranger in an expensive sports car was hard to resist. Russ was a sucker for flashy city women and he knew it. He never learned, not even after Deirdre.

The door to the post office swung open and she emerged, looking like a bird of paradise hatching in a sparrow's nest. Sonny Fouts, coming out of the hardware store, paused to stare at her, but she didn't seem to notice as she strode up the sidewalk, her briefcase swinging at her side, a cell phone glued to her face as she carried on an animated conversation.

Russ sucked in his breath as he surveyed her from the ground up, starting with the pair of dark green high-heeled boots with a row of fringe that swung to and fro with each bouncy step. Her snug black skirt skimmed over trim hips and stopped well above the knees, revealing sleek, slender legs. Above the skirt she wore a short suede jacket bearing an abundance of snaps and more streamers of fringe. Her hair tumbled in luxuriant black waves from beneath a beret.

Most people in Linhart wore hats—straw cowboy hats in

the summer, felt in the winter, and gimme caps from the feed store. But not berets. Way too French for a town founded by German immigrants. Way too citified.

"Oo-ey, she's somethin' else, eh?" Bert said with his usual candor. "Kinda on the skinny side, maybe. Uh-oh, look out, she's headin' this way."

Bert quickly picked up a three-day-old newspaper and pretended absorption in it. Russ walked casually to the back of the store to check on the coffee, facing away from the door as if the lady didn't interest him much. It was a lie, of course. Her type *always* interested him.

Russ resisted the urge to turn around when the jingling doorbell announced the arrival of a customer. He heard the rustling of Bert's newspaper and the halfhearted thumping of Nero's tail against the wooden plank flooring.

"Help you, missy?" Bert asked politely. "Bert Klausen, at your service."

The woman dropped her cell phone into her purse. "Hello, Bert." The voice was honey-smooth, confident. "Yes, I'm sure you can help me. I was told I could find Russ Klein here."

Something inside Russ jumped at the realization that this bird of paradise was looking for him. He turned around, schooling his features. "I'm Russ Klein."

She smiled a hello, and he forgot any rational greeting he might have summoned. Lord, what a smile. What a face. She made him think of an impish angel in dress-up clothes as she came toward him with her arm extended. Her hand was cool and delicate when he shook it, the long nails painted a pumpkin color. He didn't squeeze too hard for fear he'd break something.

"What can I do for you?" he asked when he'd recovered

enough of his wits to speak. Bert watched from the corner of his eye, pretending renewed interest in the newspaper.

"My name is Sydney Baines," she answered in an accent just shy of exotic.

Oh, hell. The woman had left several messages over the past few days, identifying herself as a private eye and claiming she had an "urgent matter" she wanted to discuss. Russ had ignored the calls, thinking it was a scam. What legitimate business could a P.I. have with him? He lived an uncomplicated life.

She extracted a black wallet from her green suede purse and snapped it open so that he could examine her credentials.

Russ studied the ID: Sydney Baines, Licensed Private Investigator, New York City. Now her accent and her mode of dress made more sense. And the fancy car.

"You came all the way from New York to find me?"

"I tried calling, but my messages went unreturned," she said, not a hint of censure in her voice. "It's very important that I talk to you."

"Want some coffee?" he asked, putting off whatever business she had with him. He had a feeling he wouldn't like what she'd come to say. Was some long-lost acquaintance of his mother's hoping to get a handout? They'd be mighty disappointed. The quarter-million dollars—his mother's divorce settlement from twenty years ago—was long gone.

Sydney smiled reassuringly. "I'd love some coffee." Then she lowered her voice to a husky whisper. "Is there someplace private we can talk?" She gave a tiny nod toward Bert, who continued to scrutinize the old paper as if it contained the world's secrets.

"I can take a hint," Bert said. "I'll just unpack those new camp stoves that came in earlier." With that Bert shrugged into a threadbare jacket and ambled toward the back of the store, disappearing into the storage room.

"Have a seat by the stove." Russ nodded toward the cozy sitting area Bert had just vacated, figuring he might as well get this conversation over with. "I'll bring the coffee. Cream? Sugar?"

"Cream, please." Sydney made her way toward the two wooden chairs by the potbellied stove.

Russ kept a wary eye on her as he rummaged around for two clean cups. She was on her phone again, talking and nodding as she slipped her arms out of her jacket, revealing a silky green blouse that draped over lush, round breasts. She gazed at the wide array of camping gear. Because the store was small, Russ utilized every nook and cranny to display backpacks, sleeping bags, tents and all manner of gadgets. He hung kayaks, canoes and bicycles from the ceiling.

Finally she concluded her call, sliding the phone into a jacket pocket. "This is quite a place you have," she commented. "You could buy just about anything—" Her voice broke off. "Oh, a dog."

"He's not for sale," Russ said. But when he turned back toward Sydney with the coffee in hand, she wasn't smiling. In fact, the supremely confident expression she'd worn earlier had fled and she was sitting stiff as a pine plank in her chair as Nero sniffed enthusiastically at her boots.

Russ brought the coffee over. "Nero, go lie down."

The old dog looked at Russ with a surprised expression, then ambled over to his customary place by the stove and settled down with a huff. But he continued to watch Sydney with almost as much interest as Russ felt.

"Are you afraid of dogs?" Russ asked, handing Sydney a

cup of coffee with cream. "'Cause old Nero here is about as vicious as a butterfly."

"I'm not exactly afraid of dogs, I'm just not a dog person," she said decisively, her enormous melted-chocolate eyes still fixed on the bloodhound. She was probably hoping Russ would send Nero outside, but Russ wasn't about to submit the arthritic old dog to the chilly, damp weather when he didn't have to. Not even for a pretty stranger.

Despite her denial, Russ knew the woman's aversion to Nero was more than a simple preference. She was afraid. Probably afraid of bugs and snakes, too, and he was sure her dainty little hands had never baited a fishhook with a nice, fat, slimy earthworm.

Her cell phone rang, playing a snippet of something jazzy. She checked the caller ID but didn't answer, choosing instead to turn her attention back to Russ.

He sat close enough to her that he could detect her surprising, spring-morning scent. He'd expected a woman like her to be wearing something stronger, one of those expensive designer perfumes that grabbed you by the throat.

Deirdre's perfume had been that way. And why was he thinking about *her* all a sudden? Just because Sydney was obviously a sophisticated urban woman was no reason to compare the two. Deirdre was ancient history. Sydney was here and now, and he was more than curious about her reasons for seeking him out so persistently.

Sydney pulled off her beret and hung it on the back of the chair. A wavy strand of her hair fell across her cheek, and Russ felt the illogical urge to smooth it back from her face. Before he could do something foolish, though, she tucked the hair behind her ear.

Taking a sip of coffee, Sydney pulled her scattered thoughts together. She really wasn't comfortable around dogs, especially big dogs like this one. They were dirty and smelly and noisy. She wondered how the health department would feel about one in a general store. But that wasn't her problem.

Edward Russell Klein was her problem. Or maybe the answer to her prayers.

She studied him silently. He was about the right age, thirty-two. She hadn't expected him to be quite so gorgeous, however. Even in a plaid flannel shirt and worn, soft-looking jeans that molded to his backside, he could put any of the Gucci-wearing men she knew in New York to shame. Being a wilderness outfitter must work the muscles, she mused, because he had firm, taut ones in all the right places.

She liked his hair—thick, wavy, a bit long, light brown and streaked by the sun. She couldn't exactly see him visiting a salon for highlights.

Sydney's face grew warm as she realized she'd been staring at him rather rudely.

"Is something wrong with the coffee?" he asked.

"Hmm?"

"You did say cream, right?"

"Oh." She took another sip, wondering at her lack of composure. "It's very good, thank you." He was probably used to women staring. What red-blooded woman wouldn't stare?

He took a long sip of his own coffee. "Well?" he said, sounding more bemused than impatient. He gazed at her, waiting. His eyes were a vibrant sky-blue, deep and unfathomable.

*Wrap your mind around your business, Syd.* "The firm I work for, Baines & Baines," she began, "specializes in matching up unclaimed property with the rightful owners. I believe I've found a small sum of money that might very well belong to you."

"Small, huh? Do you always travel all the way from New York for small sums of money?"

"Actually, I was visiting an aunt in Austin," Sydney said smoothly even as she upped her respect for Russ Klein's intelligence. He wasn't some country bumpkin she could easily dazzle. "But I thought I could take care of this while I'm here. If you could answer a few simple questions, we might be able to settle this matter and you could have a check in your hands very soon."

"What's in it for you?" Russ asked. His tone wasn't exactly confrontational, but neither was it warm and friendly.

"Baines & Baines works strictly on a commission basis, which means you won't owe us any money until we recover funds for you. If you're the person I'm looking for, you simply sign a contract authorizing me to claim the funds on your behalf and entitling the agency to a percentage of anything we recover."

"How big a percentage?" Russ asked suspiciously.

"Ten percent. It's actually quite low. Most other P.I.'s in this business charge far more." In this case, Sydney had deliberately decided on a low commission, not wanting to take the chance of another investigator undercutting her.

Not that any other heir-finders were on Russ's trail. She'd happened, quite by accident, onto the information that had led her here. A very different case had taken her to Las Vegas, where she'd been checking into the legality of a certain contested marriage that had taken place in a wedding chapel now known to have performed numerous fraudulent weddings. She'd nearly fainted when she'd stumbled across Sammy Oberlin's name. For years, investigators had been trying to track down Sammy's mysterious son, known only as Russell. But only Sydney had the lead—the name of Sammy's first "wife," Winnie, never legally married to him, who may very well have borne him a son.

The trail had led to Texas.

Russ made no comment. He simply studied her every bit as frankly as she'd done him. Her face felt warm, but maybe it was simply being too close to the stove. It wasn't as if she'd never received attention from a handsome man before—though not lately. For the past few months, trying to take care of her father's agency, as well as her own business, she'd barely had time to brush her teeth, much less nurture a social life.

Finally Russ spoke. "As far as I know, I haven't misplaced any money."

"That's the thing," she hurried to explain. "Most of my clients don't realize they're due some money. Sometimes it's a bank account that's been forgotten or a utility deposit. But most often, I search for missing heirs. Sometimes when people die with no will or an old or bad will, it's a real chore to locate the heirs."

"Are you saying someone died and left me some money?" He didn't look as pleased by that possibility as most people were.

Sydney didn't answer his question. Instead she said, "It's not prudent for me to reveal too many details until we have an agreement."

"Oh, I get it. You're afraid I'll cut you out."

Yes, exactly. He'd figured out her game pretty quickly. "Mr. Klein, I deal in information and information has value. Surely you can see I wouldn't have much of a business if I gave away information for free."

He continued to scowl suspiciously at her. She hadn't yet seen him smile.

"I provide a service," she continued, trying to make him understand. "I reunite people with money and property they never even knew about. And for that, I charge a fee."

Finally, his frown faded to something more like thoughtfulness. She released the breath she'd been holding. Maybe she'd gotten through.

"I don't begrudge your right to make a living however you see fit," he finally said. "But I don't think I'm the person you're looking for."

"But you don't even *know* who I'm looking for," she pointed out. What was the deal with this guy, anyway?

"Doesn't matter. I don't want more money. I make a comfortable income and I have everything I need."

For a moment, Sydney just stared. "You mean, you won't even answer a few questions?" She'd never had *anyone* refuse to let her hook them up with their money, not unless they already had an idea of where the money was. Most considered the sudden appearance of an heir-finder a gift from on high.

"I'm a very private person. I don't like people poking around in my personal life."

"Just one question. Please. Is your mother's name Winifred? Or anything similar?"

"My mother's name is Vera."

Sydney sagged. So he wasn't the right one. "And your father? What's his name?" she asked, just to be sure.

Russ's expression became suddenly fierce. "I don't have a father. My mother's never been married."

"I'm sorry, I don't mean to be so nosy, but do you at least know his name?"

He rubbed the tops of his thighs, looking out the window. She knew she'd made him very uncomfortable, but she had to be thorough.

"My mother slept with a lot of men," he finally said.

"I'm sorry," she said again. If Russ didn't even know his father's name, it was doubtful the father even knew of his existence. Damn, she'd been so sure she was on the right track. She had some other Russell Kleins to check out in neighboring towns, but this one had been her top candidate. He was the right age. Winnie's son was most likely between thirty and thirty-three. If she couldn't find him in this general area, she would have to widen her search to all of Texas—or the whole darn country, if it came to that. But that would take time and time was a luxury she didn't have.

"I'm sorry you came all this way for nothing," Russ said, and he seemed to relax slightly. "Could I buy you lunch? The Cherry Blossom Café across the street makes a mean chicken-fried steak, so at least you won't leave Linhart hungry."

She struggled to regain her equilibrium. "No, thanks," she said brightly. "Do you know any other Russell Kleins, perhaps relations of yours? Or any Winifred Kleins?"

"This town is full of Kleins. You can't hardly throw a rock without hitting one. But I don't know any others with the names you mentioned."

"Well, if you think of anyone, would you let me know? And maybe you could ask members of your family if they know. I'll be staying at the Periwinkle Bed & Breakfast."

"You're staying here?" he asked, surprised.

"I'm going to spend some time going over documents in your courthouse—birth and death certificates, property records, that sort of thing. Not all records are available online.

I'm also going to be tracking down a few more Kleins in neighboring towns."

"You could still do with lunch."

She couldn't deny that the offer tempted her. But she was on a tight schedule. She couldn't leave her father alone for more than a couple of days, not when he was in such a fragile mental state. Although his depression had lifted somewhat, he still had bad days when he needed her close by.

"I appreciate the offer," she said. "Maybe another time."

She stood and picked up her things, keeping an eye on the dog, who was still watching her with unnerving intensity. She thanked Russ Klein for his time and headed for the door, deciding quickly on a new strategy. "Oh, Mr. Klein?"

"You can call me Russ."

"Russ, then. This sum of money we're talking about. It might interest you to know that it runs into eight figures."

Russ Klein's jaw dropped and his eyebrows rose so high they almost met his hairline. Finally she'd gotten a reaction out of him.

"That's ten million," she supplied.

"I can count the zeroes. Ten million? Dollars? *That's* what you call a small sum of money?"

"Call me if you have any ideas." She hurried out of the store, resisting the temptation to stay and press the matter. Let him sit on *that* information and see how long he claimed he didn't want or need more money. Maybe he wasn't the Oberlin heir. But she had this nagging sensation he knew something and just wasn't telling her.

## Chapter Two

Russ blinked a couple of times as he tried to wrap his mind around ten million dollars. This had to be a mistake. Only one person ever in his life had that kind of money and there was no way...

When his vision cleared, Sydney was gone. The jingling of the bell on the door announced her departure. He resisted the urge to chase after her and demand to know more. That was exactly what she wanted and he wouldn't give her the satisfaction. Instead, he moved to the window to watch her walk to her car.

She had quite a nice hitch in her git-along, as Bert would say. As she started to climb into her car, a gust of wind caught her hat and snatched it off her head. She pirouetted gracefully, managing to catch the beret with both hands just before it sailed out of reach. At the same time her eyes caught his and she tossed him a wave and a mischievous smile.

How had Sydney tracked him down? When Sammy had sent him and his mom away, he'd done everything possible to erase every trace of their presence in his life.

A whine and the clicking of toenails on the wood floor

brought Russ's attention back to Nero. The dog was on his feet, sniffing furiously around the legs of the chair that had been Sydney's, then on the floor where her purse and brief-case had been.

"Don't worry, Nero, she's gone," Russ said in a soothing voice.

The dog hardly looked relieved. He pressed his nose against the wood floor and traced an invisible trail that mean-dered toward the door, his floppy jowls puffing out with each breath. Then he stopped, sniffed mightily into the air and gave a sharp bark.

"What's wrong with you?" Russ wondered aloud. The city girl had certainly played havoc with his own senses. Maybe her intriguing perfume, which lingered in the air, had upset Nero's equilibrium, as well.

After a few more anxious sniffs, however, Nero padded to his spot by the stove, plunked himself down and promptly went to sleep.

Bert emerged from the storage room, frowning. "Why did you lie to that girl?"

"Why did you eavesdrop on my private conversation?" Russ shot back, though he'd known that was exactly what Bert would do. As dear as he was, Bert was insatiably curious and a terrible gossip.

"I didn't listen on purpose, just picked up a word now and then. And the issue is you're lying. Thought you knew better."

"I didn't lie. My mother's name *is* Vera. Vera Edwina." But mostly known as Winnie.

"You're splittin' hairs. We both know the girl was talking about Winnie. She probably just assumed Winnie was short for Winifred. Which means she was looking for you."

"I don't want to be found," Russ said flatly. Not even by a gorgeous city woman with big brown eyes.

"She's gonna figure it out," Bert said. "All she has to do is ask the right person. Ten minutes in this town and she'll find out your mother goes by Winnie."

"I didn't think she'd be staying around long enough to ask," Russ said. He realized now that his strategy of misleading Sydney Baines would only delay the inevitable. "I definitely didn't know she was staying at the Periwinkle." Fortunately, the two elderly maiden sisters who ran the B and B in their Victorian home were certifiably dotty. They could cook up a wonderful breakfast, but they lived a good deal in the past and nothing they said made much sense.

"I'll just have to keep an eye on her," Russ said. "I'll make sure she doesn't talk to anyone who knows Mom."

"I don't get it," Bert said. "Didn't that purty gal say she wanted to give you money?"

Apparently Bert hadn't heard Sydney reveal the exact amount. Thank God for small favors. If Bert knew Russ was turning his back on ten million dollars, he would call the men in white coats. And maybe he *was* crazy. But he had his reasons. "Money doesn't solve all problems," he said. "And for some people, it just creates more."

"Ah," Bert said, nodding, finally getting it. "You're right about that. If you want to stop that gal from finding out the truth, you better get over to the Periwinkle and keep a watch on her."

Russ nodded. "You'll mind the store for me?"

Bert shrugged. "Like I got anything else to do?"

"And you won't say anything to Mom, right?"

"Mum's the word."

Russ wished he could take more comfort in Bert's promise

to keep quiet. But Bert kept his cell phone charged and ready, just in case he had a juicy tidbit to pass along. He had little else to do but watch who came and went on Main Street.

As Russ walked the five blocks to the Periwinkle B and B, he formulated a strategy for dealing with Sydney Baines. If she wanted to bury her nose in the courthouse records, there was no harm in that, he supposed, since the records were in such a jumbled mess she probably wouldn't be able to find anything. But he ought to take some precautions, just in case.

Maybe he'd volunteer to help her look.

The prospect of spending more time with Sydney wasn't at all unpleasant. She was the brightest thing to enter his store all winter. Maybe that single dark curl of hair would escape and fall across her cheek again. And maybe next time he saw it there, he would give in to temptation and smooth it back.

"IS EVERYTHING SATISFACTORY?" asked Miss Gail Milhaus, one of the owners of the Periwinkle Bed & Breakfast. Or maybe it was Miss Gretchen. Sydney had a hard time telling the septuagenarians apart. They were identical twins who dressed in identical vintage outfits, complete with matching barrettes in their long, silver hair. They also had a pair of identical cats that liked to wrap themselves around first one set of ankles, then the other.

"It's a lovely room," Sydney assured her hostess, reaching down to pet one of the cats. She didn't trust dogs, but cats were okay.

The misses Milhaus had made her feel very welcome. Since it was the off-season she was the only one staying at the B and B. She'd also gotten a very good room rate, almost as low as if she'd stayed out at the motel on the highway. But here she got to sleep in a soft bed with a feather comforter, take a bubble bath in a huge, claw-foot tub and enjoy a gourmet breakfast in the morning.

Sydney wasn't really much for fussy Victorian decor. She didn't like clutter and bric-a-brac, and her apartment back in Brooklyn could be described as minimalist. But her room in the B and B, painted shell-pink and featuring an abundance of cabbage roses, had a certain charm and, thanks to a crystal bowl of potpourri, it smelled wonderful.

"You look so like Miss Moony," said Gail—or Gretchen. "Are you here for the boat races?"

Boat races? This time of year? "I'm doing some research," she said. "Actually, I'm looking for a man."

The elderly lady clicked her tongue. "They're a waste of time, you ask me. Gretchen and I have lots of boyfriends, but it never works out in the long run. We've always been so close and men don't like that."

"Well, I agree, men are a lot of trouble," Sydney said with a smile. "But I'm not looking for a boyfriend. I'm trying to locate a man who has come into an inheritance. His name is Russell Klein."

"An inheritance? How exciting. And my goodness, there's that nice Mr. Klein who runs the general store and rents out the canoes and such. Could he be the one?"

"Unfortunately, I've already talked to that Russell. I don't believe he's the man I'm looking for. The one I want has a mother named—"

The sound of the door chime interrupted her. Gail stepped out of the room and looked down the stairs. "Gretchen, are you getting that?" When her sister didn't respond, she said, "Excuse me, I'll have to get the door. Perhaps it's one of our suitors."

Sydney smiled after the woman turned away. They were such nice Southern ladies—but a bit unhinged. She doubted they would have any useful information for her.

She unpacked her small suitcase. She hadn't brought a lot of clothes with her, only enough for a couple of days. If she didn't find Sammy Oberlin's heir in that amount of time, she would have to admit defeat and return to New York.

What a picnic that would be, breaking the news to her father that he was going to have to declare bankruptcy.

When she was unpacked, she opened her briefcase, tucked her small suede clutch inside and headed downstairs. She wanted to get to the courthouse right away. When she'd talked to a county official on the phone yesterday, he'd admitted that their records were a terrible mess and that only the last five years' worth had been put on computer. That meant hours of digging. Actually, she didn't mind that type of work. She was fascinated by the details of people's lives, the births, the deaths, the weddings. Old photos and diaries always sparked her imagination, causing her to speculate what people's lives had really been like.

At the bottom of the ornate, carved-oak staircase, Sydney skidded to a stop. Russ Klein was standing in the entryway, chatting amiably with Miss Gail.

"Oh, there you are," he said, flashing a dazzling smile at Sydney. "I thought since you were new in town, you might like a tour." Apparently the lure of ten million dollars had changed his tune.

She might have overplayed her hand, revealing to Mr. Klein—Russ—the amount of money involved. But she'd needed to shake him out of his complacency. And given his sudden appearance, maybe she'd done just that.

Even if he wasn't the right Russell, if he did help her locate the heir, she'd be happy to donate a portion of her commission as a finder's fee. He was probably counting on that.

Miss Gretchen joined her sister. "Oh, it's Mr. Jones, the man from the post office. How nice to see you."

Miss Gail turned to Sydney. "You won't get a better tour guide than Mr. Jones here." Miss Gail said. "Excuse us, will you? Sister, we'd better see to the horses."

"Oh, yes, indeed," Miss Gretchen agreed, and they bustled off, arm in arm.

"The horses?" Sydney asked. "What century are they in? And why does she call you Mr. Jones?"

Russ shrugged. "Last week I was Curtis. Don't worry, they're harmless. So how about the tour?"

"That's very generous of you, but I really don't have time to be a tourist," she explained. "I only have a couple of days to spend in Linhart and I need to get to the courthouse this afternoon."

"I'll walk you there, then," Russ offered. "Gil Saunders, the county records clerk, is a good friend of mine. We go rock climbing together. I'll make sure he gives you the access you need."

Rock climbing? Yeah, she could see that. Russ Klein in shorts and a T-shirt, clinging to the side of a cliff, muscles bulging as he—

*Get a grip, Sydney.* "I'd appreciate your help, thanks." Sometimes government officials could be difficult, so if Russ was willing to grease the wheels for her, she'd let him. "Let's go."

Sydney headed for her car, but Russ merely stared in amazement. "You're going to drive to the courthouse? It's only a few blocks."

Sydney considered her high-heeled boots. They weren't the best for walking and she was just getting used to the luxury of driving everywhere in a place where parking was plentiful and free. But she could survive a few blocks and the drizzle was giving way to sunshine. She put her keys back in her briefcase.

"Lead the way."

As they headed down the brick walkway toward Gibson Street, Sydney couldn't help but smile. "Those Milhaus sisters are a couple of characters," she said to Russ. "Imagine, living in that great big house your whole life, never marrying, never going out on your own."

"I don't think either of them could bear to leave that house. Their great-grandfather built it and it's been in the family ever since."

The Periwinkle wasn't the only Victorian on Gibson Street. The wide avenue was lined with grand homes, all of them painted in vibrant colors and many of them with signs out front indicating they were also bed-and-breakfasts.

Russ pointed out some of the more historically notable homes and who lived there now.

"It seems strange to me," Sydney said, "knowing so much about your neighbors. I barely know the names of the people who live right next door to me in New York."

"One reason I would never live in a big city," Russ said.

"So you're here to stay?"

"You couldn't pry me away from this town. I go to Austin or San Antonio out of sheer necessity sometimes, but other than that, everything I need is right here."

Sydney nodded in reply. Russ did seem to belong here, despite the fact he didn't talk with the native twang most of the other residents had.

"Did you go away to college?"

"Nope. I took some classes at the Boone County Community College, but I figured I didn't need a degree to do what I wanted to do, so I never got around to graduating."

"So you've always worked at the general store, doing the wilderness-outfitter stuff?"

"Worked at the store since I was fifteen. I started out just renting a couple of canoes and serving as a guide, and it grew from there. I bought the store from Bert about six years ago so he could spend his retirement fishing. But he can't stay away from the place—I think he gets a kick out of telling me how to do things."

Sydney couldn't imagine living that kind of life. It was so different from everything she knew. Yet part of her found it appealing. Her life was so hectic, so overscheduled. The closest she ever got to the wilderness was sitting on a park bench and feeding the crumbs of her cream-cheese bagel to the pigeons.

The Boone County Courthouse sat in the center of a small town square. Constructed of limestone, it was three stories tall, with a clock tower as a fourth level. Sydney consulted her slim gold watch. "The clock keeps good time."

As if on cue, the clock chimed the hour. It was one, and Sydney hadn't had lunch. But she was used to skipping meals. She was usually just too busy to eat.

"I'm turned around," Sydney confessed. "Where's Main Street?"

"The north side of the square. The general store is on Main about three blocks east. Sure you don't want some lunch before you get to work?"

There were several cute little restaurants with colorful awnings lining the square. Somewhere, someone was grilling meat and it smelled like heaven.

"Maybe something quick," she said.

"How about a sausage on a stick? Best German sausage you'll ever eat."

"Okay."

Russ led them to a little German deli, where he ordered two sausages to go. They took them to a bench on the square and sat. Sydney was glad Russ had brought lots of napkins. But despite the mess, she found it quite pleasant, sitting with the sun warming her face, sharing conversation with her host. He'd certainly thawed out. He hadn't scowled at her once since he'd arrived at the B and B. Maybe his initial coolness was just a small-towner's natural caution with strangers from the city.

She again wondered why he was going to the trouble of helping her out. Surely he wasn't this accommodating to every stranger who arrived in Linhart.

It had to be the money. In her experience, money was the prime motivating factor in most people's lives. Well, that and sex. And Russ…hmm. Was it possible he found her attractive? He'd certainly been watching her attentively. She'd made it clear she was leaving in a couple of days, but maybe he thought she would be up for some easy, no-strings sex. Living in a small town, it was probably impossible to have any kind of sexual liaison with another local, at least not without long-lasting repercussions.

Not that she ran around having casual sex right and left, but she did like the anonymity of the city. She certainly never ran into any of her ex-boyfriends—the city was just too damn big.

Well, just because she was from the city didn't mean she was easy. If Russ had a quick roll in the hay in mind, he would be disappointed. Not that the idea was without merit. And not that she'd mind the flirtation while she was here.

"Linhart is really a very nice town," she said.

"You sound surprised."

"It's a lot prettier than some of the other towns I've seen, that's all." Not that she'd seen all that many. She'd been to her father's hometown south of Austin only once, but that was more than enough. Talk about depressing.

Sydney finished her sausage and her bottled water, cleaned her hands with a moist towelette and reapplied her lipstick. Russ watched this process with undisguised interest—and perhaps a little amusement.

He threw their trash away in a nearby litter bin. "Ready?"

She nodded, feeling the first curls of temptation in the pit of her stomach. She *could* hook up with Russ. What harm would it do? She'd had virtually no social life since her mother died; even most of her girlfriends had quit calling because they'd become tired of her turning down their invitations to dinner, movies and parties.

Though she spent a lot of time with her father, she was lonely. She and Russ *were* both consenting adults.

He raised one eyebrow in a look that told her he was reading her thoughts. And that was enough to bring her back to her senses. She had work to do, a last chance to save her father from himself. Besides, she really wasn't the kind of woman who slept with strangers. As soon as she got back home, she would call some of her friends and initiate a few outings, maybe have dinner with the downstairs neighbor who'd invited her out a couple of times. Otherwise she would have to get a cat and start going by "Miss Sydney."

# Chapter Three

Russ couldn't believe the mess the county records were in. There'd been a flood a few years ago and volunteers had carried the files out of the basement willy-nilly in boxes and stacks so they wouldn't be destroyed. They'd returned the records to the basement after the flood, but nobody had bothered unpacking the boxes or refiling the records.

Gil Saunders, the county records clerk and a good friend, had shown Russ and Sydney to the basement. "Sometimes I can find things, if you know exactly what you're looking for," Gil told Sydney. "I've got some high-school kids lined up to help me get this mess organized, but they won't start till next month."

"I wish I could tell you exactly what I'm looking for. But I'm not sure. I just need to browse."

"Have at it, then."

When Sydney had gone to the ladies' room, Russ had taken Gil aside and explained to him that it was important Sydney never locate any records having to do with him or his mother.

Gil, a real friend, didn't even ask why. He quickly gathered up the few things he could lay his hands on—Russ's mom's business license and the deed to her little house—then took them to his office and hid them in a drawer. Unfortunately, that was all he could do. He couldn't guarantee Sydney wouldn't come across something in the old records, but the chances of her finding what she was looking for in this mess were minuscule.

Sydney, on the other hand, saw the basement as a personal challenge. "Just stand back and watch," she said with a grin. "If there are pertinent records to be found in here, I'll find them."

She actually seemed to like groping around in the mildewed boxes and dusty drawers, and she did seem to have a knack for knowing which piles of records would yield Kleins.

Still, after almost four solid hours of this tedious, grimy work, broken only by frequent trips upstairs to check her cell phone, which didn't get a signal in the basement, she'd found absolutely nothing that pointed to the Russ Klein she was looking for. Thank God.

She was clearly disappointed and Russ felt bad for her. Of course she would be disappointed, getting so close to a million-dollar commission she was unable to collect. He didn't feel bad enough, however, to help her out.

In fact, he was probably doing her a favor. Everyone thought being an instant millionaire would give them a dream life. Russ had the personal experience to know it could just as easily ruin a life.

The sun was already setting as they exited the courthouse. "So what are your plans for tomorrow?" Russ asked as they headed back toward the bed-and-breakfast.

"I'm going to track down every Klein family in this area and talk to them personally," she said. "Someone, somewhere, must have heard of this Winnie Klein."

Russ cringed. Any person passing on the street had probably heard of Winnie. He needed to get Sydney Baines out of this town, somehow. Which gave him an idea.

"You know, I've been thinking. I have a little cabin not far from here. It's just a hunting cabin in the woods, but there are a whole bunch of family papers stored there—boxes and boxes of photo albums and letters and I don't know what all. You're welcome to look through those. It's possible the people you're looking for moved out of the area. Or this Winifred person could have gotten married out of state, changed her name. Maybe you could uncover some clue."

He could see that the idea appealed to her. But she hesitated. "I should talk to your mother. She might remember—"

"No, I wouldn't waste your time there," he said firmly. "Mom knows nothing about her family history. My grandparents were divorced and she never really knew anyone on the Klein side of the family." All of which was true.

"Then who does this cabin belong to?"

"A cousin on my grandfather's side." Bert actually was a very distant cousin, if you went back about six generations. "I got to know him pretty well, and he gave me a key to the cabin."

"You're kind to offer to let me look, but I have some appointments tomorrow morning in Longbow and Conklin. More Russell Kleins. They're all too old to be the heir I'm looking for, but they might have relations the right age. But if I still have no information by tomorrow afternoon, I'll give your cabin a try."

Good. Longbow and Conklin were nearby, but not close enough that the residents would know Winnie, not unless he was truly unlucky.

"I'll be at the store whenever you're ready to go."

"If nothing turns up, I'll come by around one o'clock."

"And what about tonight? Any plans?"

"I'm going to wash all this grime off me, then I'm going to do some reading."

That wasn't the answer he wanted. If she spent the entire evening at home with the Milhaus sisters, Winnie's name might easily come up.

He feigned shock. "What? You're only here for a couple of days and you're going to spend the evening reading?"

"What can I say? I don't lead a very exciting life."

"I could change that. Do you like to dance?"

"I'm not a good dancer," she said warily.

He didn't blame her for being cautious. His actions this afternoon could be interpreted as merely friendly. He'd done nothing to indicate he was romantically interested in her. But now he was veering into boy-girl territory. He'd asked her out on a date.

As pretty as she was, she probably got hit on constantly.

"You don't have to be a good dancer to have fun, especially country-dancing," he said. "There's a club over on Highway 350 that has a pretty good band on Thursday nights."

He could see she was tempted.

"We could have some Mexican food beforehand," he added. "I'll take you to a place where they have the best tamales in the whole state. Bet that's one thing you can't get in New York."

Finally she smiled. "Okay, you got me. How can I resist the best tamales in Texas? But, Russ, if you have any plans for us… You know the kind of plans I mean?"

Oh, yeah. "A guy always has plans. Do you have a boy-friend back home?" Or even a husband. She didn't wear a wedding ring, but these days that was no guarantee.

"No, but…I just want to keep things light."

"No problem, Sydney. I'm pleased just to have your company for the evening, no expectations."

"Okay, then. Pick me up in an hour. What should I wear?"

"Jeans. Comfortable shoes."

"I didn't bring either."

He shrugged. "Improvise. This club doesn't exactly have a dress code."

RUSS KLEIN was a gentleman, Sydney would give him that. He arrived exactly on time, and though he eyed her skirt and blouse dubiously, he said nothing. At least she'd worn her lowest pair of heels, in case she actually got up the nerve to dance.

She was almost disappointed Russ didn't drive a pickup. She thought every good Texas boy drove a truck. Instead, his vehicle of choice was a Bronco. It was shiny and clean and smelled nice. Even better, though, was the music: he was playing Stevie Ray Vaughan on the stereo.

"You like Stevie?" she asked.

"I'm surprised you even know who Stevie is."

"My father is from Texas. He made sure to teach me all about the Texas blues."

"You might actually like this band tonight, then. It's not the usual twangy country stuff, though that's good, too."

Tia Juana's Tamale Factory was a hole-in-the-wall in a strip shopping mall. But the parking lot was packed and when Russ opened the door the smell that greeted Sydney made her mouth water. They found a table and Russ went up to the counter to order for both of them.

The other patrons who crowded into the place were a real cross section. Sydney saw working men in their overalls, young couples all dressed up for a night on the town and senior citizens. As in New York, multiple cultures and languages mingled easily, sharing a common love for good food. She was used to thinking of Texas as almost another world and was surprised at the reminder that people were the same everywhere.

"Popular place," Sydney observed when Russ returned.

"You'll know why when you taste the food. It's also cheap. Uh, which is not to say I wouldn't have spent more on you."

"Oh, so you're a smooth talker." She suspected he was putting on a bit of an act for her, but she responded to it anyway.

When they called Russ's name and he went to collect their food, he returned with a tray loaded with a mountain of Tex-Mex.

"Oh, my gosh. Where do you start?" she asked.

"Anywhere you want. Just dig in. I got lots of everything, so there's bound to be something you like."

After sampling the guacamole, the crunchy beef tacos and the shredded chicken tamales, Sydney declared that she liked it all. "I'm not going to fit into my clothes if I keep eating like this."

"We'll work it off dancing," he said.

If the restaurant wasn't exactly classy, the club was downright questionable. Russ pulled up to a barn-sized corrugated tin building with a flickering neon sign that read Kick 'em Up Club. The dirt parking lot was filled with beat-up trucks and motorcycles. If the handful of kids smoking near their bikes was any example, Russ in clean jeans and shirt was on the elegant end of the dress scale.

A three-dollar cover charge got them inside. Sydney almost laughed: if you wanted to hear live music in New York, you had to pay at least ten.

The inside of the club was like a big cave. Tables and chairs were arranged haphazardly around the dance floor and a bar lined one long wall. Onstage, the band was just getting set up, but a jukebox pumped country twang into the beer-rich air.

"We better grab a table fast," Russ said. "This place gets packed when the Jimmy LaBarba Band plays."

"Hey, Russ, over here!" A couple of guys were waving to Russ from a table already crowded with beer bottles.

"Do you mind sitting with some friends?" Russ asked. "We can get our own table if you want."

"No, let's sit with a group." That way, it would seem less like a date.

The group consisted of two couples who were kayaking buddies. It seemed whatever the outdoor activity, Russ was involved. Cycling, hiking, swimming, windsurfing—he did it all. The other couples were friendly to Sydney and she made herself relax and go with the flow. It had been so long since she'd socialized with people her own age and it felt really good just to kick back and enjoy herself.

Russ hadn't exaggerated—the band was good. Sydney was familiar with most of the songs, covers of her dad's favorite artists like Lyle Lovett, Delbert McClinton and Omar and the Howlers. But they also played a few original songs and Sydney was impressed enough that she bought their CD as a present for her dad.

After a couple of beers, the band had launched into a set of more traditional country fare. The music was a little more dance-friendly.

"What do you say?" Russ asked. "Want to give it a try?"

"Okay." What the heck. If she made a fool of herself, it didn't matter. She'd never see these people again.

She soon knew she'd made a mistake. Russ was a good

dancer and before the end of the first song he had her two-stepping like a pro. But the feel of his hands on her—he held one of her hands and put his other on her waist—left her flushed and breathless.

When the band started a slow song, she knew she should insist they take a break. But she didn't. She let herself go into his arms, let herself rest her head against his shoulder.

It felt so good, better than anything she could remember in a long time, and she knew she would think about this night a lot in the days to come and the longing to be with him again would consume her.

The party broke up relatively early, it being a weeknight and all of them having to work the next day. The band was still going strong, though, as they left the club.

Russ held her hand as they walked across the parking lot to his car, ostensibly to guide her around the many potholes. But she liked the feel of it.

"That was really a lot of fun," she said as he drove her back to the B and B. She half hoped he would ask her to go home with him. As vulnerable as she felt, she might have succumbed to the temptation. But he honored her request that they keep things light. He walked her up to the front door of the B and B.

"You have a key?"

"Oh, yes. Miss Gail and Miss Gretchen made a point of informing me that they went to bed promptly at nine o'clock and after that I was on my own till morning."

"They're nice ladies. And they cook a mean breakfast."

"Oh, no, I can't even think about more food! I'm still stuffed from dinner."

"Make room. The sweet rolls are not to be missed." He

kissed her once on the cheek and then very lightly on the mouth. It wasn't nearly enough. "Good night, Sydney."

"'Night."

She watched him through the window as he walked back to his Bronco with that loose-limbed gate, and couldn't help regretting what would never be.

AT A LITTLE BEFORE ONE O'CLOCK the following afternoon, Sydney returned to Linhart. Every lead she'd followed that morning had been a bust. She had two choices: concede defeat or take Russ up on his offer to go through the papers at his cabin. Defeat wasn't an option.

A bunch of papers in an old cabin was a weak lead, but she wasn't exactly depressed by the work that lay ahead. She was curious to know more about Russ and his family. Last night he had deftly sidestepped any questions she'd asked about his relatives, but he'd done it so smoothly she hadn't really realized it until later, when she'd lain in bed dissecting the date.

Most people loved to talk about themselves. And while she guessed Russ really was a private person, she still had a hunch he was hiding something. But why would anybody hide from ten million dollars?

She knew her way through the town now, and she reached the square and navigated the one-way streets to get to Main, again marveling at what a pretty town Linhart was. A new, quaint scene greeted her around every bend. The town could have been mistaken for an Alpine village and the German influences were unmistakable: the Willkommen Guesthaus, the Dietzel Microbrewery, the Schnitzel Haus Family Restaurant.

Sydney pulled up to the curb in front of the general store, parking neatly between two trucks. If there was one thing she could do, it was parallel park, though her old Volkswagen Beetle back home was a lot easier than the beemer she'd borrowed from her aunt Carol. Sydney had been a bit nervous about driving the luxury car, but Carol, who lived in a fancy retirement community in Austin and seldom drove her car, had insisted she borrow it rather than getting a rental.

Given the state of Baines & Baines's accounts, Sydney had readily agreed. After her mother's death, her father, Lowell, had fooled her into thinking he was doing okay, but eventually she'd discovered the state of his finances. If she'd known how bad things were, she could have intervened sooner. Now, unless she could track down the elusive heir, it was too late for the business.

After exiting the car, Sydney made a final check of her appearance, smoothing the olive wool skirt over her hips and adjusting the collar of her black silk blouse. Maybe the zebra-stripe jacket was a little flamboyant for small-town Texas, and it was true she hardly needed it—the weather had improved a great deal from yesterday morning's dreary drizzle, but it matched her long scarf and she was a sucker for matching accessories.

When she reached the general store's front door and opened it, she found Bert sitting by the stove again, crunching on another pickle. He was just the sort of quirky old man you'd expect to find in a small Texas town. He was thin and slightly stooped, with wispy silver hair and sharp blue eyes that missed nothing.

"Hello, again," he said without much enthusiasm

"Good morning," she said as she strolled in, bringing a gust of wind with her. "Where can I find Mr. Klein?"

"He's busy right now," Bert replied, not meeting her gaze.

Was she imagining things, or was the man just a little hostile toward her today? "I told him I might drop by around one," she said, checking her watch. It was five minutes after. "But I don't mind waiting a bit if he's busy."

She would wait as long as she had to, since she had no other leads to follow. She could have flown back to New York today, but she'd already paid for the extra night at the Periwinkle.

Besides, if she were honest with herself, she wanted to see Russ again.

Bert sighed impatiently. "He's in back gettin' some supplies ready for a camping party. You can go through the storeroom and out the back door, if you want. But I think you should know—he makes a terrible boyfriend."

"Excuse me?"

"Just a word to the wise. I've seen the city girls come and I've seen 'em go. He might look like a good catch, but unless you like fishing and camping, you're not likely to see much of him. And if you have any notions about dragging him to the city and putting him in a suit, you might as well give up right now."

Sydney resisted the urge to laugh, because Bert was obviously sincere. He was trying to protect his friend from what he saw as a predatory female, an evil city woman.

"My dealings with Russ this afternoon are strictly business," she said.

"That's not what I hear."

Oh, dear. She hadn't meant to become the center of gossip. Another reason she liked the big city. No one cared whom she dated; no one paid attention to what time she came home or even *if* she came home. Not unless she counted her father, who'd developed an unnatural dependence on her lately. He'd already called her twice this morning with problems at the office he wanted her to solve. He'd made it clear he wanted her home—yesterday.

Bert returned to his newspaper, but Sydney could tell he was still watching her suspiciously. She made her way across the wood floor, around the counter and into the storage area, feeling Bert's gaze burn between her shoulder blades the whole way.

The large storeroom was lined with all manner of products, from canned peas to laundry detergent to cat food. Stacks of camping gear—tents, sleeping bags, lanterns, cooking utensils—covered the floor. Big canoes hung from hooks in the ceiling. A thick steel door to the outside was unlatched and only slightly open.

Sydney peered through the crack, catching sight of Russ before he saw her and pausing a moment to savor the sight. She had to admit, he was one of the most attractive men she'd ever come across. His image had remained firmly implanted in her mind long after he'd dropped her off last night—hair with streaks of burnished brass and eyes the same color as a clear winter sky. He again wore faded jeans and much-laundered flannel shirt that revealed firm muscles every place she looked.

That rugged, outdoorsman look fit him as gracefully as the tailored-suit look fit some other men she knew.

As he leaned over to drop an armload of gear onto a blue tarp, his shirt stretched invitingly across wide, powerful shoulders. Sydney could easily guess what that soft flannel would feel like, how the firm body beneath the fabric would react to her touch.

She'd been thinking about it—had thought of little else, really, even when she'd been tracking down long-shot leads. She'd pretty much decided they'd done the right thing last night. One or two nights with this man would never be enough, yet anything more permanent was out of the question for her right now with her home in New York and her father depending on her. She couldn't possibly maintain a relationship with a man who lived half a country away from her.

Russ turned to pick up a cooler and caught sight of Sydney. Immediately his chiseled features rearranged themselves into a smile. As he came closer, she caught a hint of his intriguingly masculine scent.

"Any luck with the other Russells?" he asked.

"Nothing but dead ends. Your cabin full of papers and photos is sounding better and better. Have I come at a bad time?"

"I have to get all the supplies ready for a camping party that's set to show up any minute."

"Need some help?" she asked. "I can tote and lift."

He gave her a skeptical look. "I can handle it, if you don't mind waiting a few minutes."

"Please, go ahead. I noticed a historical museum on the next block. That looks interesting. The curators at small museums are often a wealth of information. Maybe I'll just run over there—"

"No." He said it, so emphatically she jumped. "I mean, the guy who takes care of the museum will talk your ear off about everything you don't want to know about and it's hard to get away from him. If you'll just wait a few minutes, I'll be done here and I can devote my full attention to you."

"Well, okay." But she still thought the museum sounded interesting. And talkative people were lifeblood for a private investigator like herself. She'd never had any problems with people who talked too much, only with people, like Russ, who kept their mouths shut. Fortunately, there were a lot more talkers in the world than silent types.

She found a perch on the edge of a concrete planter and watched him work.

He disappeared into the storeroom and returned with a tent, a lantern and some other items Sydney didn't recognize.

After his third trip, a battered pickup truck bearing four boisterous college kids whipped into the parking lot.

Sydney waited patiently while Russ dealt with them, answering yet another call from her father, who couldn't resist checking up on her every few hours. Ever since her mother's death, her father relied on daily pep talks from Sydney to keep him going.

"I wish you'd tell me what you're up to down there," he huffed.

"I told you, I'm following a lead. It could mean a good commission. I'll tell you more about it when I know more." Lowell would freak out if he knew she had a lead on the Oberlin case. It might be just the thing to blast him out of his depression, but her likely failure might make things worse. "Aunt Carol is doing well."

"There's something you're not telling me," Lowell Baines concluded.

Darn it, even in his depressed state, his instincts were sharp. It was almost impossible to fool him. "I have to go, Dad. I'll be home soon. Love you."

"But, Sydney—"

She disconnected. Otherwise he would keep her on the phone forever, pestering her.

Russ was piling gear into the bed of the pickup and answering questions about terrain and the weather forecast, which was apparently of some concern. Although the sun was shining now, rain was due to move into the area that evening and

Russ gave careful instructions for preventing the tents from washing away.

During one of his trips between the storeroom and truck, a sleeping bag toppled from his arms. She retrieved it for him and carried it to the pickup while the college boys eyed her breasts. Russ shot them a look that ended the ogling.

His display of primitive protectiveness made Sydney's blood sing through her veins. She was looking forward to getting his "full attention."

## Chapter Four

Russ hurried to get the college kids on their way. So far he'd lucked out. The Milhaus sisters hadn't revealed anything pertinent. But he had trouble on another front. His mother had heard about his date with Sydney last night, not to mention that several people had seen them yesterday around the square.

"If she's your new girlfriend, I want to meet her!" Winnie had insisted when she'd called that morning. He probably should have seen this one coming.

"She's not a girlfriend," Russ had assured his mom. "She stopped by the store and we struck up a conversation. It's just a casual thing and she's leaving in a day or two. I'll probably never see her again. You wouldn't like her, anyway." Which was blatantly untrue. His mother liked everybody. She'd always gotten on well with Russ's girlfriends.

But in this case, the ends justified the means. Winnie had wasted too much of her life focused on money, had practically ruined her life in the pursuit of it. The one time she'd had money of her own, after Sammy paid her off to disappear, she'd blown it all on every unhealthy pursuit imaginable.

She was happy now, doing a job she loved and living

close to people who cared about her. But that would change, he knew, if she saw a chance to get her hands on more of Sammy's cash. The mere whisper of millions of dollars would send her into a tailspin he didn't care to witness or deal with.

He glanced at Sydney; she was sitting on the edge of a planter with her face to the sun, enjoying the gorgeous afternoon. What had started out as a simple decision on his part to refuse an inheritance had turned into a big pile of deceit, and he didn't like that, or himself for that matter, one bit.

Still, he only had to keep the two women apart for another day or so and his problems would be over.

He approached Sydney, who had her eyes closed. "Hello?"

She jumped. "Oh. Sorry. I was about to doze off. I'm afraid I didn't sleep too well last night."

He hadn't, either. He kept thinking about Sydney in his arms, how she'd felt, how she'd smelled, and he'd lain awake for hours. He wondered if her sleeplessness had a similar source and couldn't help hoping so. "Was there a problem?"

"It was too quiet," she admitted. "I'm used to traffic noises at night and all I could hear were my own ears ringing from the loud music at the club."

So much for his fantasy that she'd been desperate for his touch.

"You actually like the city noise? I guess you can get used to anything." He remembered what it was like to sleep in their Vegas apartment. Though he and his mother had lived in a pricey complex, the walls were paper thin. All night long, he'd hear people coming and going, cars and sirens, drunk pedestrians outside and his mother's partying friends inside. He couldn't imagine how anyone found that preferable to peace and quiet.

He looked down at Sydney's feet. "We'll have to do something about your shoes."

"Why?" She looked down at her black, pointy-toed heels. "I won't actually have to hike into the woods, will I? I have a policy never to walk on dirt." She laughed, but Russ didn't join her. They would, in fact, have to hike to get to the cabin, but he didn't want to scare her off.

"What size do you wear?" he asked.

"Six-and-a-half," she answered. "But—"

He went inside and Sydney followed, looking troubled. He scanned the shelves of shoeboxes until he found what he wanted, then grabbed a pair of socks. "Try these on."

With a shrug, she slipped out of her heels and put the socks and hiking boots over her stockings.

Russ watched, appreciating the curve of her calf and her dainty ankles. She must really want to get at those papers, because she wasn't built for outdoor adventures.

Nor did she dress for them. Today's hat was some high-fashion take on a pith helmet. But as he watched her stretching to lace the hiking boots, he had to revise his initial impression. Beneath the olive skirt and zebra jacket she was no city-girl softie. He saw muscles in those legs.

Forcing himself to look elsewhere, he grabbed a couple of backpacks from the storeroom and quickly filled them with a couple of days' food—easy stuff that wouldn't require a lot of preparation. The cabin had a pantry full of canned and dry goods, so she wouldn't starve. He included some bottled water.

While he worked, Sydney tried out the shoes in the main area of the store, pacing along one aisle and down another, her hips swaying gently with each step. Not that he was watching.

"These are really comfortable," she said when she returned to the storeroom. "I'll take them."

"Consider them a gift," he said. A guilty gift. Not that an expensive pair of hiking boots would make up for the hoax he was about to perpetrate. "Are you ready?"

She grabbed her purse and briefcase. "Sure." He didn't deserve the warm smile she gave him.

Bert agreed to watch the store the rest of the day, though grudgingly. He probably thought Russ had fallen for the bird of paradise, and it wouldn't be the first time.

His last three girlfriends had all been city girls, two from Austin and one from San Antonio. None of them had been compatible in the long run, though for a while he'd thought Deirdre was the one. They'd been unofficially engaged and he'd designed his house with her in mind—someplace spacious and comfortable where she could feel at home. But before he'd laid the foundation, she confessed that she couldn't survive in a small town, that she would go crazy with boredom. She'd been certain she could persuade him to move to the city.

That's what happened with all of them. As soon as the novelty of tiny Linhart wore off, they couldn't return to the bright lights fast enough. They couldn't believe that he stayed in Linhart out of preference. It was as if deep down they believed he was just sitting there, waiting for the right woman to come along and save him from this small town.

He kept telling himself that a plain, uncomplicated, salt-of-the-earth farm girl would be his ideal mate—someone with old-fashioned values who appreciated the things he did. Problem was, he had yet to meet one around here who stirred up even a single hormone.

By contrast, Sydney stirred up a whole flock of hormones. Could he help it if he was a man who appreciated beauty in its more exotic forms?

Out behind the store, Russ opened the passenger door of his Bronco. He honestly tried not to watch as Sydney vaulted gracefully aboard, but he couldn't miss the glimpse he got of the top of one stocking.

The woman wore real stockings, with a garter belt. That brief glimpse was going to haunt his dreams for a long time.

By the time he slid behind the wheel, Sydney was already sifting through his CDs, which was just as well. He wouldn't have wanted her to notice that he moved a bit, well, stiffly. He set two bottles of water in the cup holders and revved up the Bronco's engine.

"You've got some great stuff here," Sydney said, selecting an early Lyle Lovett album. "You and my dad should compare notes some time."

He doubted he would ever meet Sydney's father. But he was probably an interesting man, given how his daughter had turned out.

Russ pulled out of the parking lot and down the alley, checking the clock. They had plenty of time. They would arrive at the cabin well before dark, provided Sydney took to hiking.

They cruised down Main Street. Russ took the scenic route, making a few extra turns. He felt a weird compulsion to show off his adopted hometown. He pointed out a few of the sites she'd missed yesterday, like the Linhart Winery.

"Do they import wine?" she wanted to know.

"Of course not. We grow the grapes not far from here. Every bottle of wine they sell is one-hundred-percent Texas."

"Texas wine, huh?"

She sounded dubious, but it was no use arguing. "You'll have to taste it some time. It's good." Finally he headed for the highway out of town. "If your father is a Texan, how'd you end up in New York?" He was genuinely curious why anyone would leave the Lone Star State for noisy, smelly New York. This place, with its ever-changing landscape of hills and forest, canyons and rivers, vast fields of wildflowers and winding, scenic drives, was paradise on earth as far as he was concerned. It had always felt more like home to him than Vegas.

"My father's the one who left, not me," Sydney explained. "He fell in love with New York and moved there before I was born, thank God."

"Why, *thank God?*"

She laughed. "Can you imagine me with a Texas accent?"

"So you must really love New York." He had no reason to feel disappointed, but he did.

"Oh, I do. Theater, museums, subways and taxis, Central Park, the Statue of Liberty. In New York, every day's an adventure."

"You can find adventure here," he said, not sure why he was trying to convince her. It was her business if she wanted to breathe pollution every day and fall asleep to the sound of sirens and horns at night. But it was best to keep her talking about *her* family and off the subject of *his*. "So where's your mother from?"

Sydney blinked rapidly and for about half a second her face reflected a brand of deep grief Russ was pretty sure he'd never felt. He'd obviously stuck his foot in it and was searching for something to say when she spoke.

"My mother was pure Manhattan," she said, her voice cracking. "She died a few months ago—almost a year, now.

She was my father's business partner. They formed Baines & Baines together when they were hardly more than kids."

"Baines & Baines," Russ murmured. "I thought *you* were one of the Baineses."

"Not officially. I started out working for the family business, but then I branched out on my own. Heir-finding is fun, but it's mostly research and phone calls. I wanted to get out in the field a bit more, so I started handling other kinds of cases and eventually set up my own office in the spare bedroom of my apartment."

"But now you're heir-finding again?"

"Temporarily. I'm helping out my father. Mom had the business head in the family and I'm afraid Dad has made rather a mess of things. I'm trying to get everything sorted out and keep the business on an even keel until he's ready to take the helm again." The note of cheerfulness she'd injected into her voice rang false.

"I'm sorry about your mom." That wasn't anywhere near adequate, he knew, but he wasn't good with words or warm fuzzies. He spent too much time alone with his hound dog and with gruff Bert for company.

"No, *I'm* sorry," Sydney said with a self-conscious hand to her forehead. "I didn't mean to get sidetracked into my problems."

"What type of cases do you handle when you're not helping your dad?"

"A lot of security-consulting work. I have all kinds of clients—everything from mom-and-pop grocery stores to casinos. I do some insurance fraud, your garden-variety background checks on prospective employees, the occasional cheating spouse."

"Sounds like your dad is lucky he has you to step in when he needs help."

Sydney huffed. "You'd think that, wouldn't you? But for Dad, I'll always be a little girl. He checks up on me every five minutes."

And solving this case—finding the long-lost Sammy Oberlin heir—would impress the hell out of her old man. Russ could read between the lines. That was why she was pursuing the case. Well, that and the million-dollar commission.

"Why does the conversation keep turning back to me?" she asked, sounding put out. "I'm the one who's supposed to be asking the questions. What can you tell me about this cousin of yours?"

If he kept changing the subject, she would get suspicious. So he gave her some of the truth. "He's an older man. A widower. Has some kids and grandkids. His family goes back at least four generations in the Linhart area."

"Have you ever heard of him talk about relatives in the Las Vegas area?"

"Not that I recall." Russ needed another distraction to delay Sydney from interrogating him. Otherwise, he was going to have to lie outright to her and he didn't want to do that. "Are you hungry?"

"After the breakfast I had at the Periwinkle? Not likely. By the way, you were right about the sweet rolls."

"Then would you mind reaching around to the cooler behind my seat and getting a snack for me? I haven't had lunch."

"Okay, sure." She unfastened her seat belt and twisted her body around so she could lean between the bucket seats. Her skirt rode up on her thigh and Russ drank in an extended, appreciative and unapologetic look. Her legs were long for such a petite woman and she definitely had good muscle tone.

"Do you want pretzels, an apple or a granola— Oh, yuck!" She pulled back and rubbed furiously at her face. "That dog is in the car. He stuck his tongue in my ear." She sounded utterly disgusted.

With a sinking stomach Russ glanced over his shoulder. He hadn't planned on this outing being a threesome. Sure enough, though, Nero crawled out from under a tarp in the backseat. At some point when Russ had turned his back—probably when Sydney was distracting him—the sneaky old hound had climbed into the back of the Bronco so he could come along for the ride.

Nero shoved his head between the bucket seats and madly sniffed at Sydney, who had her hands protecting her face from his inquisitive tongue.

"Nero, go lie down," Russ said in a loud, stern voice.

The dog gave him a surprised, injured look before reluctantly retreating to the cargo area behind the backseat.

"He's gone now," Russ said to Sydney.

She started digging in her purse for something. "Does he go everywhere with you?"

"Most places," Russ answered. "But today he's a stowaway. I think he likes you."

"Likes me? He tried to take a bite out of my ear."

Russ looked over at Sydney's pink shell of an ear, which certainly didn't bear any teeth marks. "In twelve years, Nero has never bitten anyone. He's not about to start with you. He *licked* your ear." Maybe the dog liked the body lotion she used. Russ himself wasn't immune to her delicate scent and thought that licking her ear wouldn't be a bad place to start.

"He was tasting me," she insisted. She'd found a moist towelette in her purse and was energetically washing the side of her face, her neck and any other place with which Nero might have come into contact.

Russ sighed and tried to drag his gaze back to the road, which wasn't easy since she was wiping her cleavage. He was pretty sure Nero hadn't licked there.

Still, the Nero incident was a perfect reminder. Just when he was starting to like Sydney, she gave him another reason why he shouldn't.

"What sane person doesn't like dogs?" he couldn't help asking. "What's not to like? Dogs are the ultimate embodiment of unconditional love. Even if I've only been gone ten minutes, Nero greets me like a long-lost friend. He lives for someone to scratch him behind the ears or give him a doggy treat. Dogs have simple needs." Not like women, he almost added.

"You can save your breath. No private detective likes dogs."

From the corner of his eye, Russ noted the rise and fall of her chest. His initial guess had been correct. She was *afraid* of dogs.

He shrugged. At least Nero's timely show of affection had taken Sydney's mind off Russ's family.

"Do you still want a snack?" Sydney asked, regaining her composure.

"That's okay. We'll be at our destination before too long, and I'll grab something then."

She tugged down the hem of her short skirt and put her seat belt back on, peering over her shoulder every so often to ensure the dog remained in the cargo area.

"How come you're so afraid?" he asked.

"I told you, I'm not afraid of dogs. I'm just not fond of them."

"So you've never been bitten?"

She hesitated. "Well, yeah, I was. Just one more reason not to like dogs. You can't trust them. They may fool you into thinking they're domesticated, but one false move and they'll turn on you."

"How old were you when you got bitten? Or was it more than once?"

"Once was enough," she said with a shiver. "I was five. A neighbor's chow jumped me when I was riding my bike down the sidewalk. He'd always been friendly before that."

Russ knew about dogs and bikes. He'd been chased down a time or two by territorial farm dogs. "A moving bicycle awakens some dogs' prey instinct. The chow probably thought you were a very large rabbit."

"Exactly my point. At any moment, they can revert to the wild."

"So can people," Russ couldn't resist pointing out. He'd seen enough dog-eat-dog behavior in Vegas to convince him of that. "But that doesn't mean you should dislike and avoid all people."

"I'm sure your dog is a sterling example for the whole species, but I still don't trust him. I'm sorry if that hurts your feelings."

Russ laughed. "It's your loss, missing out on the love of a good dog. That's okay. Both Nero and I still like you."

She eyed him curiously, apparently not sure how to take his flirting. When he grinned back at her, she looked away.

Another spear of guilt needled him. What kind of a degenerate flirts with a woman he's lying to?

"Did the chow hurt you badly?" he asked, feeling sympathy for the small child she once was.

"I spent a week in the hospital and another three years in and out of surgery."

"Oh, I'm sorry, I didn't mean to make light of it." No wonder she didn't trust dogs. No wonder she was afraid—even if she refused to admit it. He glanced over at her, giving her a frank examination. "I don't see any scars." At least, none that weren't covered up by clothing.

She reached over, took his right hand off the steering wheel, and placed it under her hair at the back of her neck. "Feel the bumps?"

He nodded, running his fingers along her skin as if he were reading braille. Bumps or no, her neck felt nice.

"I wear scarves for a reason. But I did have an exceptional doctor. He got rid of most of the scars."

"But not the ones in here." He lightly touched her temple, then quickly returned both hands to the steering wheel where they belonged.

"Dogs sense something in me—hostility, maybe. I give off some scent only they can smell. If I walk into a pet shop, all the dogs start barking like they have rabies."

"Nero likes you. Why else would he kiss you on the ear?"

At the sound of his name, the dog's head popped up from behind the backseat. Sydney stiffened, though she said nothing.

"Nero, lie down."

Nero's hopeful eyebrows fell as he disappeared once again behind the seat. Sydney relaxed.

Figuring they'd talked enough about dogs, Russ kept Sydney distracted by pointing out a landmark here and a rock formation there. She responded with seeming interest, sometimes asking a question or simply nodding thoughtfully.

"It's beautiful out here, even in the winter," she conceded. "Even a confirmed urbanite like me can appreciate that."

After they'd been driving for about twenty minutes, Russ

pulled off the main road and onto a rutted dirt road that challenged the Bronco's suspension. Five minutes later, he stopped at a washed-out bridge that had once spanned Deer Creek, a ribbon of water with a steep, rocky bank.

Stately oaks, scrubby mesquite and maples crowded the road from both sides and climbed the distant hills, their brown, bare trunks interspersed with evergreen junipers. One thing Russ loved about the Hill Country was the way the landscape varied from bare, brown rocks to gentle hills and valleys coated with buffalo grass to lush woods.

"Wow." Sydney gazed through the windshield at a landscape that was picture-postcard perfect, even when the trees were bare of leaves. "Is this a state park or something?"

"Actually, it's private land owned by some hospitable friends of mine," he said as he cut the engine. "But it butts up against a park creating an uninterrupted chunk of wilderness." Big enough to support some of the threatened animals that needed large areas to range, like bobcats and cougars. But he wisely chose not to mention critters of any kind to Sydney. If she was afraid of old Nero, he couldn't imagine how she would react to a cougar.

"Have we stopped here for a reason?" Sydney asked.

"No bridge."

"Can't we…go around?"

"Sorry, but from here we have to hoof it."

"What? How far?"

"Only about four miles." Not giving her a fair chance to object, he opened his door and jumped down, leaving her gaping.

# Chapter Five

Sydney shut her mouth. Four miles? Why was she panicking? She could do four miles. In New York terms, that was forty blocks. She walked that far some days. And on the treadmill, she ran as many as five or six miles. Piece of cake.

Anyway, she had a feeling Russ enjoyed forcing her out of her comfort zone. She wouldn't give him the satisfaction of knowing he'd startled her.

Sydney opened her door, looked down at the red mud, grimaced and jumped down. Her feet sank into the soft earth and she was grateful for the hiking boots. Her suede, high-heeled shoes would have been instantly ruined.

It felt good to stretch her legs after the cramped confines of the truck. It was actually a pretty big truck, but it had *felt* cramped, given the two overwhelming presences she'd been forced to share it with. Just the thought of that beast lurking in the back made her break out in goose bumps. As for Russ— well, his presence was threatening in an altogether different way. Unfortunately, she didn't feel like hiding from him; in fact, she'd had no trouble confiding highly personal information, especially strange for her given that she was usually slow to trust strangers.

She closed the door to the truck and stretched her arms up over her head, taking in a deep breath of country air. Lord, what she wouldn't give to have this quality of air where she lived.

A sharp bark startled her and she whirled around. The dog was still safely confined in the back of the Bronco.

"He just wants to get out and explore," Russ said from behind the truck. He opened the rear door.

Sydney shuddered and stepped to the other side of the road, where she wouldn't have to look at the beast. While Nero explored, Russ turned his attention to hauling out a couple of backpacks.

"What do we need those for?"

"It's always a good idea to be prepared when hiking into the wilderness."

"Please don't tell me the dog is going to hike with us."

Russ sighed. "No, he'll stay in the truck."

*Thank goodness for small favors.* Sydney might actually enjoy a nature hike, but not if she had to worry about a dog putting his muddy paws all over her or slobbering on her clothes. Besides, dogs were genetically wolves. In the wild like this, wouldn't it be easy for one to revert? And Nero was big, maybe bigger than a chow.

"He might like to come with us," Russ continued, "but I don't take him hiking anymore. Last time I did, he took off after a rabbit and didn't come home for two days. When he finally showed up he was more dead than alive."

The dog kept his nose to the ground, checking everything out, then came to the exact spot where Sydney had stood and sniffed the ground madly. Nero then followed her trail around the Bronco and stopped right in front of her, giving a sharp bark. Sydney cringed. The beast was hunting her. Why couldn't Russ see that?

"Nero!" Russ called, and the dog went to his master's voice. Russ loaded him back into the cargo area. He opened all the windows a few inches, then locked the dog inside.

With Nero taken care of, Russ shouldered his backpack with economical movements, then nodded toward Sydney's. Determined to rise to whatever challenge he placed before her, she shrugged into the pack, then let Russ adjust the straps, aware of his strong, capable hands, brown from the sun even in winter. When he readjusted the collar of her blouse, his fingers brushed against bare skin and she shivered.

"Cold?"

"A little," she fibbed. Actually, she was warm, verging on hot, thinking about the feel of those hands against her skin. *Just move a little to the left....*

The pack adjusted to his satisfaction, he stared at her an uncomfortably long time, as if sizing her up—or maybe guessing her lascivious thoughts. She hoped not. "Is it too heavy?" he finally asked.

She took a few steps, getting used to the weight. "I can handle it."

Russ raised an appreciative eyebrow, but said nothing.

Sydney, who'd never hiked in the country or gone camping her whole life—and who'd never had a desire to do so—was actually looking forward to the hike now. She wanted to show him she wasn't some pampered princess. Even if she didn't like walking on dirt.

Russ led the way down the steep bank to the edge of the creek bed, offering a hand to help Sydney. She shook her head, then wished she hadn't been so proud when she slid partway down on her butt. Thankfully, he didn't see her lapse in grace. But her skirt was probably ruined.

They walked alongside the creek for a while, then crossed to the other side on a natural bridge formed by a tree trunk. This time, she didn't hesitate to take the hand Russ offered. No way was she going to fall in a cold creek, even if it looked to be only a few inches deep.

The climb out of the creek bed was easier and from there they took a rough footpath through some scrubby trees. The path wasn't difficult, and Sydney was able to fully enjoy her surroundings.

The scenery was breathtaking, with sheer limestone cliffs, pockets of heavy woods and open areas of barren rock. For most New Yorkers, her included, Texas evoked images of deserts. Cactus. Ranches and oil wells. She'd been to Austin a number of times to visit Aunt Carol, but she'd seldom ventured beyond the city limits before this trip. She never would have guessed she would encounter this kind of scenery.

The sounds of the wind in the trees, the chatter of birds, the crunch of dead leaves under her feet—they were all foreign yet intriguingly familiar to her. Surely she'd soon tire of a steady diet of this Daniel Boone stuff, but one afternoon wouldn't hurt her.

They passed a waterfall that emptied into a deep, mysterious looking pool and Sydney thought about how refreshing it would be to swim here on a hot summer day.

She wondered if Russ ever swam here. And if so, did he skinny-dip? Her face heated at the mental image taking shape and she shook her head to banish it before she became so distracted she smacked into a tree trunk.

As they topped a grassy rise and entered a meadow, Russ dropped back to walk next to her. "Tired?"

"No. I'm used to walking. At home, sometimes it's faster than braving the traffic. Disappointed?"

He grinned. "You must really want to see those papers."

She did. And yet she wasn't all that optimistic about what she would find. Russ said he hadn't gone through the boxes. For all anyone knew, they could be filled with old newspapers or recipes.

What was the real reason she'd been so eager to accompany Russ to his cabin? And why hadn't she asked him more than a few superficial questions?

She knew the answer, she just hated to admit it. Russ had already told her his mother's name was not Winifred. Didn't that take him out of the running as the Oberlin heir? She should have returned to San Antonio and resumed her search. She had a few more Russell Kleins to go through.

But she wasn't done with *this* Russell, not yet. She wasn't done fantasizing about him. She hadn't gotten her fill of his muscular body, his clear blue eyes and the way his mouth creased at the corners when he smiled, which wasn't often enough. She hadn't seen enough of the way he moved, so much a part of this wild environment, yet achingly human and all man.

They walked on in silence for a while. They'd been hiking for almost forty-five minutes when Sydney detected a sound, something new, something distinct from the pleasant din of the woods. She looked up into the trees and saw nothing out of the ordinary. She looked from side to side, still seeing nothing. Finally she glanced over her shoulder.

Oh, for heaven's sake. The dog was loping along the trail behind her, panting happily.

"Russ? Excuse me, Russ?" she called out.

Russ stopped and turned. "Problem?" Then he spotted his dog. "Nero, what are you doing here?"

"Can your dog open car doors?" Sydney stood still as the dog sniffed her boots.

"He must have squeezed through one of the open windows."

"If he gets those muddy paws on my skirt, I'm sending you the cleaning bill."

"The skirt's already ruined," he pointed out. "I'll buy you a new one."

Darn it, he'd noticed her clumsy fall after all.

Russ pulled a piece of rope from his backpack. He tied one end of the rope to Nero's collar and yanked him away from Sydney. "What's gotten into you, boy?" To Sydney he said, "I guess we have no choice but to take him with us. I hope I don't end up carrying him back."

Sydney pictured Russ hiking back to the car with the big dog on his shoulders. He probably wouldn't hesitate to do so. Clearly, he was ridiculously fond of the beast.

Yet another reason she should keep her distance. As if she needed more reasons.

Russ slowed his pace slightly, remembering he had a greenhorn with him. Sydney, however, showed no signs of fatigue. She wasn't even breathing hard, though her face was pleasantly flushed from the mild exertions

But the trail got rougher from that point on. They were hiking more or less parallel to Deer Creek, which had cut a small canyon in the limestone as it wound down the hill. They made several more crossings, sometimes using log bridges, sometimes hopping from rock to rock.

They paused at a particularly difficult spot, where the trail narrowed and climbed almost straight up for several yards. Russ pushed Nero up ahead of him, then doubled back to give Sydney a hand. As she scrambled up, a branch knocked her hat askew.

When she reached the ledge where he was standing, he straightened her hat. And there was that lone curl, dammit, dangling against her cheek.

If anything her face turned a darker shade of pink. Suddenly all he could think about was how it would feel to kiss her, to crush those full, soft lips with his and kiss her until common sense was nothing but a dim memory.

And then he did it.

She responded like a flower to the sun, open, soft, pliant. Her arms went around his neck, her fingers twining in his hair as his mouth plundered hers. He pulled her slender, lithe body against his, feeling the heat of her, smelling the essence of her, the incredible texture of her lips.

He wanted to feel more of her hair. He plunged his hands into the thick, black mass, knocking her hat off.

She made a noise in her throat that could have been excitement, or it could have been the beginnings of an objection. Whatever, it brought him to his senses. When he ended the kiss, her reaction was immediate. She pulled away from him as if he were a hot branding iron.

"I didn't mean—"

"That wasn't supposed—"

They both started speaking, broke off, then laughed nervously. Russ took a couple of steps back, almost falling over a rock. He needed to get out of touching range.

"I didn't plan that," he finally said. "It was that damn curl that fell over your cheek. It drove me temporarily insane."

She shoved her hair behind her ears self-consciously, then retrieved her hat. It wasn't altogether useless, he realized. At least it had a small brim that shaded her face from the sun. She repositioned her pack on her shoulders and set her gaze on the trail ahead. Russ realized the subject of the kiss was closed.

"The cabin's not much farther."

During the next ten minutes, Russ kept an anxious eye out over his shoulder, but Sydney seemed to be doing fine. Still, he was relieved when they made the final creek crossing. Another hundred yards and they reached a clearing with a cabin in the center.

"Oh, wow," Sydney said, and he couldn't tell whether she was impressed or appalled.

He remembered his own thoughts the first time he'd seen it. It looked like something out of a fairy tale, made of rough-hewn logs with a stone chimney and two porches that ran the length of the whole cabin, front and back.

But no one had been up here in a few months, so it was overgrown with weeds and the front porch was covered with dead leaves. At least he didn't spot any broken windows, which inevitably led to an invasion of critters.

He climbed the stairs to the porch and unlocked the front door. The cabin smelled winter-musty, but everything appeared in order. "Take your boots off and leave them on the porch," he instructed. "No sense tracking mud everywhere."

Sydney looked at the dog, which was standing just outside the threshold, waiting for permission to enter. His feet were coated in mud. "What about him?"

"Nero, go lie down. You can't come in like that."

With a sigh that sounded decidedly human, as if he'd understood every word Russ said, Nero lumbered to a sunny spot on the porch and plopped down. He looked over his shoulder at Sydney, silently imploring her to show some sign that she didn't hate him. For whatever reason, the dog had taken a liking to her.

Sydney entered the cabin in her stocking feet. "It's really rustic." She gave a glance to the mounted deer head over the fireplace, the braided rug, the granny-square afghan on the ancient sofa. She shrugged out of the backpack and let it fall with a clunk. "You don't actually hunt, do you?" She glanced again at the deer and wrinkled her nose.

"Nah." Not since he was a kid, anyway. Bert had taken him a few times when he first moved to Linhart, but it wasn't really his thing. "I fish sometimes, but really this is just a place to get away from everything."

"I would think Linhart is far enough away from everything."

"Now you're dissing my town."

"Sorry, I don't mean to. Linhart is beautiful, really. And quiet. I just don't see why a person would need to get away from it."

"It's not so quiet during tourist season. Spring through early fall, it's wall-to-wall people." And sometimes he just needed to get away from Winnie. When she got a moneymaking idea in her head, she would pester Russ about it endlessly. She would never follow him here, that was for sure. The former Las Vegas showgirl didn't much care for walking on dirt, either.

"Do you want to see the boxes?" he asked Sydney. "They're upstairs in the loft. If my cousin ever got that space cleared out, we'd have another bedroom."

"I'm not sure why you'd need another, if you come up here to be alone."

"Maybe I won't always be alone." Maybe someday he would have a wife and kids who'd want to rough it here with him. Although, given his track record, that was becoming less and less of a possibility. He'd yet to convince any of his girlfriends to tromp up here with him—not even Deirdre. Then again, she'd worked in the governor's office in Austin and would have looked as out of place in the woods as a flamingo in a desert.

None of the other women from his past would have fit in, either. Melanie What's-Her-Name, the oil company lobbyist, had broken out in hives when he'd taken her on her first and last canoe trip. Elizabeth, the hotel events coordinator—well, he'd never even tried to picture her anywhere in the great outdoors.

Sydney was probably the only female to see this place in fifty years and she had come under false pretenses.

Still, he couldn't deny she classed the place up. Something about her was different from those ultrasophisticated women he'd been involved with in the past. Or perhaps he was merely trying to rationalize his attraction to her.

"All right, let's have a look at those boxes," she said briskly.

He led her up a narrow spiral staircase to a loft bedroom. As soon as Sydney reached the landing, she let out a soft *"oh"* of surprise.

The room was literally full of boxes, wall to wall and floor to ceiling, and every one of them filled with yellowed papers, photographs, scrapbooks, letters, postcards and who-knew-what.

"It would take me a month to go through all this stuff!"

"You can take as long as you want," Russ said mildly. "There's enough food, between what's in the backpacks and the kitchen cabinets, to last you several days. I'll come back to get you whenever you say."

"You're going to leave me here alone?" Panic edged her voice.

"I have a business to run."

"I can't stay here overnight," she objected. "I didn't bring clothes or a toothbrush or—"

"There are plenty of clean clothes in the bedroom closet

and dresser drawers, and I packed a few toiletries in the back-pack. But if you don't want to stay, I understand. We have to start back within a few minutes, though, if we want to make it home by dark."

She looked at the boxes, then back at Russ, weighing how badly she wanted to find Sammy Oberlin's heir against how badly she *didn't* want to spend the night in the woods.

"Fine," she ground out. "I'll stay one day, and if I can't find anything by then, forget it. I'm going back to New York."

Exactly what he'd been hoping to hear. But as he looked at her, standing in the loft staring forlornly at all the boxes, he felt nothing but guilt. He didn't want to leave her here alone with her work, which wouldn't lead to anything anyway. He wanted to take her downstairs, bundle her into the feather bed, burrow under the down quilts and make love to her until neither of them could move.

"I guess I better call the B and B and let the sisters know I won't be back tonight." Sydney looked around for a phone but didn't spot one. "Let me guess. No phone."

"I do come here to get away from everything," he reminded her.

"Good thing I remembered to bring my cell phone." She reached into her jacket pocket and pulled it out. She'd just bought it a couple of weeks ago, the latest and greatest on the market.

Russ eyed it with interest. "I've never seen a phone like that."

She held it out for his inspection. "Cool, huh? I can use it to read e-mail, do research on the Web, listen to music—it's an mp3 player, too. With this thing I'm always connected, always at the office. I *never* miss a call."

"Um, yeah, well, hate to break the news, but unless it's a satellite phone, you won't get service out here."

"What? That's ridiculous. Everyplace has cell coverage these days."

"Not these woods."

She checked the screen more closely. Sure enough, her phone wasn't receiving a signal. "My father will be worried sick about me if I don't call him tonight." Sydney gnawed on her bottom lip, then reminded herself to stop. It was a nervous habit she thought she'd conquered years ago.

"I can let both the B and B and your dad know where you are," Russ said.

She could just imagine. Some strange guy calls and claims Sydney is stuck in the middle of nowhere and can't be reached, but don't worry? "Why don't you call my aunt instead?" Sydney suggested.

"Sure, no problem."

Aunt Carol would be cool about it. She could keep her father calm if he got worried.

Russ wrote down the number Sydney gave him and stuck it in his pocket. "Have fun, I'll see you tomorrow."

She couldn't believe he was leaving, just like that. But she couldn't very well beg him to stay.

Russ started a generator, so she would have electricity. Then collected the dog from the porch and started the hike back to the car. Sydney watched him until he was out of the clearing, disappearing into the trees.

She felt abandoned and forlorn. When she'd first visualized herself going through all these boxes of historical papers, she'd thought Russ would be helping her—identifying people in photos or the authors of letters. It had sounded like so much fun, a treasure hunt.

Doing the job alone wasn't nearly as appealing. But she

kept the goal in mind—verifying the identity of the Oberlin heir. Maybe one of those boxes held a ten-million-dollar clue.

But before she could do anything, she had to use the bathroom. She wandered into the single downstairs bedroom, but the only door led to a closet which was, as Russ had promised, filled with spare clothes. Changing into a comfy pair of jeans and a sweatshirt sounded like a good idea—after the bathroom.

But there was no bathroom.

Sydney inspected every inch of that cabin. There was no bathroom. She ran out to the front porch.

"Russ!" she yelled as loud as she could. "Russ, come back! I have a problem!" But he must have been too far down the trail, because he didn't return. Either that or he had chosen to ignore her.

That was when she spotted a small building off to the side, shielded by some sapling trees. "Oh, no." It couldn't be. Surely she was just missing something, a hidden door or something. Surely he didn't expect her to… But, yes. As she drew closer to the small building, she saw the quarter moon carved into the door.

## Chapter Six

When Sydney saw Russell Klein tomorrow, she was going to kill him. She gritted her teeth and opened the door to the outhouse. This experience would make for an amusing anecdote to tell her father, she realized with a faint smile. If it made him laugh, picturing his purely urban daughter stuck in the boonies without a flush toilet, the inconvenience would be worth it. Almost.

In the closet back in the cabin she found a pair of jeans and a flannel shirt that were miles too big but warm and comfy. She would have to remember to take a picture of herself with her phone. The snapshot of her dressed like a hillbilly would go well with the anecdote.

Finally, she climbed the stairs to the loft, eager to get on with her task. It was hard to know where to start, so she grabbed a box at random, sat cross-legged on the floor and started digging.

The first box appeared to be filled with receipts, all dated from the 1940s. The name on each and every receipt was Bert Klausen.

Bert Klausen? She'd heard that name before, she thought with a surge of excitement. Had it come up in previous research? Then her hopes fell as she realized Bert was the elderly gentleman who'd greeted her at Russ's store, the one with the pickle.

Bert was the cousin?

She wondered what all these receipts were kept here for. Had Bert actually lived here? Obviously, because she couldn't envision anyone hauling boxes of junk through the woods just for storage.

Other boxes yielded similar fare—mail, most of it of a business nature but a lot of it just purely junk mail. Why would anyone keep junk mail? She shuddered as she thought about those people who never threw anything away, the ones who let old newspapers, magazines and empty cans stack up in their houses floor to ceiling, until only a narrow path remained leading from room to room.

Actually, her father could easily grow into one of those people if someone didn't keep tabs on him. He wanted to keep everything; he was always sure he might need it someday. In the first months after her mom died, his house and the office had become unbelievably cluttered and Sydney had to fight him every step of the way as she'd tried to purge the junk.

Lowell Baines never would have fought his wife—he knew Shirley had the business sense and had deferred to her. But Sydney was his little girl, who obviously knew nothing. He didn't trust her to make decisions about his affairs. In fact, he was still trying to make decisions about *her* life.

Finally she found a box filled with old photo albums. She loved looking at old pictures, even if she had no idea who was in them. It always made her sad when she saw photo albums at estate sales or antique shops. Hadn't some family member wanted those photos? She had loads of old albums that had belonged to her mother, each picture meticulously labeled, and she knew the stories behind them, too.

But not everyone shared her love for recording the past. These albums, for instance, were falling to pieces. Many of the old photos were faded and few had captions. The subjects that were identified featured first names only. But she did see a few photos, dated from the 1930s, with a little boy whose name was Bertram Jr. She could only guess this was the pickle-eating Bert and that the receipts had probably belonged to his father.

But no Kleins. No Oberlins. No Winnies or Winifreds or Sams.

The deeper she delved into the boxes, the more positive she became that these boxes had all belonged to Bert and had nothing whatsoever to do with Russ or any other Kleins.

She'd been had.

Why did he want her out of town so badly? What was he trying to hide?

She wasn't going to kill Russ, though. That would be too quick and easy. Somehow, she was going to make him suffer for dragging her up here for no good reason.

"Do I REALLY HAVE TO buy that expensive shampoo?" asked Sylvia Grimes. She was one of Winnie Klein's best, most regular customers. But she also asked the same question every time she walked into Winnie's hair salon, the Cut 'n' Curl.

"Darlin'," Winnie said as she used a soft brush to sweep away the last few stray hair clippings from Sylvia's shoulders, "you can use any kind of shampoo you want—if you want to be back here in a week begging for a new dye job because you look like Bozo the Clown. I know this all-natural stuff is pricey, but it's the best shampoo I've found for preserving color."

Winnie patted her own deftly highlighted locks. She did the best color this side of San Antonio, if she did say so herself. But a cheap shampoo would ruin everything and Sylvia knew that.

"Oh, all right," Sylvia grumbled, stuffing the bottle of shampoo into her bag along with one of each freebie Winnie put out for her customers—a refrigerator magnet, a key chain, a pen, an emery board and a letter opener. Sylvia must have had dozens of each by now, but every two weeks she loaded up again.

Sylvia was Winnie's last customer, thank goodness. Her other two stylists, Betty and Glory, were just finishing up with their clients.

Winnie did a tidy little business. Just about everybody in Linhart came to the Cut 'n' Curl to get their hair and nails done. Her customers tended to be extremely loyal; a few who had moved away even made the trek back to town just to have Winnie work her magic on their locks.

As Winnie changed out of her uniform, Betty and Glory swept up, readying everything for tomorrow. Winnie was straightening up the dressing room when the bell over the door rang.

"Tell whoever it is, we're closed," Winnie called out from where she was gathering used smocks to run through the washer.

"Winnie, honey, it's not a customer," Glory informed her. "It's that handsome son of yours."

Glory Dickerson had been lusting after Russ since the two of them were in high school. In fact, Winnie suspected Glory had gone to beauty school strictly so she could get a job with her, Russ's mother, and foster a connection. But it hadn't worked. While Russ was always pleasant to Glory, he'd never shown any signs of being attracted to her, despite the fact Glory was curvy in all the right places, with big green eyes and piles of long red hair.

Winnie stuffed the smocks into a laundry bag and emerged from the dressing room with a smile for her son, who offered her a dutiful kiss on the cheek.

"What's the occasion?" Winnie asked. Though she saw Russ on a fairly regular basis, he seldom dropped by the shop. The ultrafeminine decor and the perfumed air made him uncomfortable, she suspected.

Not to mention the cow eyes from Glory and every other woman under the age of fifty. But he never dated local women, preferring the glossy city girls he somehow managed to meet.

"No particular reason," he said. "I just wondered if you wanted to go out to dinner."

"Well, Russell, aren't you sweet. Of course I would love to have dinner out with my favorite son."

Her *only* son, but she was sure if she had others he would still be her favorite. When they'd first moved to Winnie's hometown of Linhart, she'd wanted to pass him off as her half brother. She could have gotten away with it, too, since her father had moved away to parts unknown when she was a baby. But Russ, only twelve at the time, had vetoed that plan. He'd insisted that since they were making a fresh start, they should start as they intended to go, by being honest.

He'd been right, of course. He'd been mature far beyond his years, and thank providence for that. If she hadn't had Russ to help her manage her affairs, she'd have blown the rest of her divorce settlement and have nothing to show for it.

Betty said her goodbyes and left for home, but Glory still

hung around, sweeping the perfectly clean floor around her chair and blatantly staring at Russ, who didn't seem to notice.

"I'll finish up here," Glory offered magnanimously. "If y'all want to beat the early bird crowd at the Cherry Blossom. They're having a special on catfish tonight." She was angling for an invitation to join them.

Russ was either oblivious to Glory's unabated adoration or studiously ignoring it.

"I thought we'd go to the club," Russ said.

Winnie smiled, pleased by the thoughtful invitation. "Sure, hon, but am I dressed okay?" She ran her hands over her tight, short skirt. She hadn't gained a pound since her Vegas showgirl days, but she had to admit that her, um, assets had shifted around somewhat.

"You look beautiful as always, Mom."

With an apologetic look, she allowed Glory to make good on her offer of closing up. She handed the laundry bag to Russ—she'd run the laundry through her machine at home later. Then she grabbed her purse and the two of them set off for the Lake Linhart Country Club, about a fifteen-minute drive away. They would be unfashionably early for dinner, but that didn't matter so much in this little town, not like in Vegas where only the people confined to nursing homes ate dinner before ten o'clock.

"You said there was no occasion," Winnie said as Russ pulled his Bronco into a parking spot. "But why is it I don't believe you?" She gasped as an unsettling thought occurred to her. "You're not getting married, are you? That woman who's been into the store the last two days in a row, the one you took dancing…is it her?"

Russ laughed. "Guess I can't make a move without you knowing. The Linhart grapevine is alive and well. But, no,

I'm not marrying Sydney. She'll be going back to New York tomorrow."

"Well, good. I mean, I'm sure she's a perfectly nice girl, but I don't understand why you don't hitch up with some nice girl from Linhart. Like Glory."

"Glory's nice," Russ said mildly. "But she doesn't do a thing for me."

"And Sydney does? What kind of name is Sydney, anyway?"

"A city name, I guess. Don't worry, she's not a girlfriend and I have no intentions toward her. In fact, she's the one pursuing me. She's, uh, kind of a stalker."

"Oh, Russ, that sounds awful. What's going on?" And why hadn't the grapevine supplied any details? Bert, whom she could usually rely on to tell her every detail of Russ's business, had remained cagily mum about the dark-haired woman's purpose in Linhart. He claimed he didn't know anything, but Winnie could tell he wasn't being truthful with her. His nose twitched when he told a lie.

Russ waited until they were seated at a white-clothed table near a wall of windows where they could watch the sun set over the lake.

"She's got a crush on me, that's all, and she's one of these girls who won't take no for an answer. So if she comes snooping around you or the shop, don't tell her anything about me. In fact, you probably shouldn't talk to her at all. Just tell her you're too busy."

"I'll do that," Winnie said. "Do you think she's dangerous? She's not one of those if-I-can't-have-him-no-one-will kind of girls, is she?"

Russ laughed. "No, it's nothing like that. She's not the slightest bit scary. In fact, she's afraid of Nero."

"That old dog?" Winnie laughed. Bert had given Nero to Russ as a gift on his eighteenth birthday. Russ and the bloodhound puppy had been inseparable ever since. He loved that old dog and would probably fall to pieces when Nero passed—an event that couldn't be too far off.

"Yeah," Russ said, grinning. "She claims she simply doesn't like dogs, but it's obvious how nervous she is around Nero. The funny thing is, Nero seems to like her."

"That is funny." Nero had never before taken to any of Russ's many female admirers. The dog didn't care much for her, either.

Winnie couldn't help wondering if Nero was echoing Russ's own feelings regarding the woman—that he liked her more than he was letting on.

"Is this woman staying in town or what?" Winnie asked. "Her BMW is still parked in front of the store, I noticed."

"She was staying at the Periwinkle, but tonight she's busy elsewhere. Not in town," he clarified. "She'll be back in Linhart tomorrow afternoon, but I think that's the last we'll see of her."

Russ didn't sound as happy about that as Winnie thought he ought to. Something more was going on here than met the eye. But if she tried to worm more information out of Russ, he would clam up. She would have to find out some other way.

The waiter came and took their order. Though the menu featured all kinds of trendy, continental dishes, Winnie ordered the fried catfish.

"If I'd known you wanted catfish," Russ said, "we could have gone to the Cherry Blossom after all."

"Yes, but we wouldn't have seen this sunset."

Russ gazed out over the lake, seeming to see the incomparable view for the first time. "You're right. God, that's beautiful. The most beautiful sunsets in the world are right here in the Hill Country."

Not that they'd seen sunsets anywhere else but Vegas. But Winnie thought her son was probably right. She couldn't imagine any place more beautiful.

"Actually, I did have a reason for taking you out to dinner," Russ said. "I want to give you a present."

"Really?" Winnie loved presents and she especially loved surprise gifts. "Any particular reason?"

"Well, your birthday's coming up next month. And I would have waited, but this was a deal too good to pass up."

He handed her a red envelope with her name on it.

With quivering hands, Winnie opened the envelope. "A whole weekend at a spa! Oh, Russ, what a thoughtful gift. And it's that fancy one in Austin—" She squinted at the card again. "But it's for this weekend."

"The sooner the better, right?"

"I'd have to leave tomorrow."

"That shouldn't be a problem. I'm sure Betty and Glory can cover for you, or you can rearrange a few appointments."

"Oh, honey, this was so nice of you, but Betty's daughter's baby shower is on Saturday and I can't miss it, I'm one of the hostesses. Maybe the spa will let me reschedule. You think they will?"

"They're always booked months in advance, is what I hear. Sorry, Mom, I didn't know about the baby shower."

"Well, I'll work something out," Winnie said, "even if I have to schedule my spa visit for next year." She stepped around the table to give Russ a hug. "This was really generous of you."

He shrugged. "It's been a good year at the store. I think as hard as you work, you should pamper yourself every so often."

"Can I get one of those mud baths?" Winnie asked. "It might be worth missing Betty's shower for a mud bath."

"You can get whatever you want."

Russ had ordered the shrimp scampi, but he hardly tasted it when it arrived. He'd just wasted several hundred dollars, not to mention the fifty bucks he'd shell out for dinner.

What was worse, tomorrow he was going to be dealing with a very ticked-off Sydney Baines. He'd forgotten to tell her about the hidden door behind the staircase that led to the bathroom.

## Chapter Seven

By early afternoon of the next day, Sydney was ready to gnaw her own arm off to escape from the cabin in the woods.

She'd nearly frozen to death last night, despite the fact she'd rolled herself up in feather comforters like a caterpillar in a cocoon. The sink in the kitchen would have featured running water if she could have figured out how to make the pump work, which she couldn't.

Last night for dinner she'd eaten all the granola bars and finished almost all the bottled water from the two backpacks. At a little after six the sun had gone down and the cabin had become pitch black—no electricity. Though Russ had started up the generator, it had conked out less than an hour after his departure.

Now, grimy from not bathing and grumpy from lack of sleep, she was resorting to the canned food she'd found in the cabinets—none of which had labels. The Texas heat had apparently melted all the glue that adhered the labels to the cans and they'd fallen off, perhaps years ago.

This morning she'd had cold barbecued beans and succotash for breakfast. For lunch she'd had a real treat—cold split pea soup and unsweetened cherries. She'd have opened more cans and hoped for something better, but with the crummy little crank can opener, the task of opening had taken her fifteen minutes per can and her hand was killing her.

She was back to wanting to kill Russ. She would wait until he'd led her out of this godforsaken wilderness. Then she would conk him on the head, steal his car and drive herself straight to the Austin airport.

She couldn't believe she'd let herself get talked into this— and all because a studly guy had flexed his muscles and batted his blue, blue eyes at her.

Yeah, killing him would be something of a waste. Maybe she'd have sex with him first.

Oh, God, what was wrong with her? She hadn't had any coffee this morning, for one thing. She'd found some coffee and an ancient percolator. But the percolator didn't have a plug, even if there'd been anything to plug it into, which there wasn't. Apparently it required a heat source and Sydney could not for the life of her figure out how to light the antique woodstove. She had wood and she had matches, but throwing matches onto the wood hadn't accomplished anything. After using up almost an entire box of matches, she'd given up.

Maybe she should have joined the Girl Guides when she had the opportunity, but the prospect had horrified her and she'd sworn she would run away from home if she had to wear one of those uniforms.

Okay, so she couldn't kill Russ, and sex was out of the question. When he finally arrived to take her back to civilization, she wasn't going to speak to him. That's what she'd do. Give him the silent treatment.

Unfortunately, when he finally did arrive some time in the

early afternoon, he found her sitting cross-legged on a sunny spot on the porch, fast asleep. She was warm for the first time since the previous day and her stomach was full. Since she was completely sleep deprived, she'd succumbed to fatigue. She'd planned on greeting him with an icy stare and a haughty sneer—not rubbing her eyes and struggling to wake up like a child awakened too soon from her nap.

"Sydney." He gently shook her shoulder. "Hey, Sydney, you okay?"

"No, I am not okay," she managed, but her voice sounded all bedroom muzzy instead of royally ticked off.

"Did you find the bathroom?"

"If you're referring to the world-class facilities over there," she said, pointing to the outhouse, "yes, I did."

"I'm so sorry. There's a bathroom inside, but I forgot to show you where it is."

"There is no bathroom in that cabin," she argued. "I checked every single door."

But when he led her back inside, he walked over to a wood-paneled wall under the stairs. All you had to do was press on it. A previously well-hidden door sprang open.

"You mean, there was a bathroom here the whole time?" She could not believe this. She'd endured that disgusting out-house for nothing!

Sure enough, the tiny bathroom featured all the amenities—well, the bare minimum, but it looked like heaven to her.

"I'm sorry," he said again. "I've never brought guests here before. I forgot the door was hidden."

"Yeah, well, you neglected to mention a few other things— like the fact I'd have to build a fire if I wanted to heat food or avoid freezing to death, or the fact I needed to know how to repair a generator."

"Something's wrong with the generator? I thought you'd turned it off."

"It quit working right after you left. And you could have warned me that sleeping would be impossible. I don't know what kinds of creatures live out here, but they were having a party and I think a bear was trying to get into the cabin. At one point I actually got up and locked myself in the closet. And they say the city is noisy."

"No bears here," he assured her.

"Then what was it?"

"Raccoon, probably, or maybe a skunk. They're always looking for a handout."

"Just get me out of here, okay?" So much for the silent treatment.

"Okay. Did you find anything in those boxes?"

"Oh, yeah, I found loads of stuff—about Bert Klausen's family. Certainly nothing about yours."

At least Russ looked a bit guilty.

"Bert's no more your cousin than he is mine. Admit it. You dragged me here to get rid of me. You're hiding something."

"Bert *is* a cousin." He didn't bother denying the rest of her accusations. Which only made her feel worse. He really *had* wanted to get rid of her. She knew she could be annoyingly persistent when she was trying to find answers while working a case, but she'd walked away from him and he'd insisted on coming after her. He'd been the one who'd invited her to go dancing. He'd pushed the idea of the cabin. Did he dislike her that much? Was he secretly contemptuous of her New York accent and city ways? Had taking her out to dinner, dancing and being nice been some sort of setup?

"We'd better start back," Russ said. "There's a blue norther' headed this way and it's gonna get cold. Might even have some ice."

"I just need to change clothes and I'll be ready to leave," she said stiffly.

"You might want to keep those clothes for the hike. Pretty as you look in a short skirt and slinky blouse, flannel and cotton are a lot more practical."

"Wear these clothes in public?" No way. This trip to Texas had been a disaster from start to finish; she wasn't about to add fashion crime to her list of faulty decisions. And if he thought flirting with her and calling her pretty would offset her anger, he was sadly mistaken.

"Suit yourself," he said with a shrug.

She quickly changed back into her skirt, blouse and jacket, immediately feeling more like herself even though she'd had to trash her stockings. She stuffed the old jeans and flannel shirt into her backpack—there was plenty of room now that she'd eaten all the granola bars and drunk all the water. She would launder the clothing and return it to Russ, showing him that she had manners even if he didn't.

She waited on the front porch while Russ closed up the cabin. The weather was still pleasant. It was hard to believe that anywhere in January could be so mild, harder still to believe a cold front would hit in a few hours. She hoped the weather didn't delay her flight. She was booked on a red-eye leaving at ten tonight. She'd be home by morning.

"Ready?" Russ asked, suddenly appearing on the porch beside her.

She nodded. She was beyond ready to get back to civilization and was feeling grateful she'd not been born a hundred and fifty years ago to a pioneer family.

It felt good to stretch her muscles after crawling around for hours the previous day digging through those boxes. And the hike was much more pleasant now that she didn't have to worry about the dog. At least Russ had left the beast at home this time. Now the only distraction was Russ himself, hiking a few feet in front of her. She wished he didn't have to be so darn good-looking. What was it about soft, faded denim over a man's posterior that was so appealing?

She stumbled and almost fell.

Russ halted and looked over his shoulder. "You okay?"

"Yes, fine," she said quickly, reminding herself she needed to keep an eye on the path ahead rather than her guide's backside.

"Looks like we had some rain last night. Just enough to make things slippery, so watch your step."

His warning came about a second too late. One moment she was contemplating what Russ might look like naked, the next, something gave way beneath her foot. With the backpack throwing off her balance just enough, she couldn't catch herself. She let out a scream as she found herself falling down a hillside, hitting trees like a pinball on the way down.

She did a neat somersault and wound up on her butt in a pile of wet, rotting leaves.

For a few moments she was so stunned she couldn't move, couldn't say anything. Then she was vaguely aware of Russ calling her name as he scuttled down the hill after her with amazing speed. He was at her side almost instantly.

"Sydney, don't try to get up."

Which was exactly what she was doing. The damp leaves

were soaking through her skirt and she didn't want to finish the hike with a wet behind. But then the pain hit. Her left ankle and her tailbone, mostly, but she'd bumped and scraped herself in a number of places on the way down.

"Are you hurt?" he asked. "Did you hit your head?"

"My ankle," she finally said, barely managing to get the words out. It felt like someone was hitting her foot with a sledgehammer. "I think I broke it."

HELL. This was exactly the kind of thing he was always cautioning his hikers to watch out for. You had to pay attention on these trails, which weren't intended for casual strolls. He should have warned Sydney to be more careful from the beginning. He probably should have checked to see that her boots were properly laced, to give her ankles the support they needed.

Getting her off the mountain and to medical help was going to be a trick, assuming he could even get them out of this gully. Doing it before the blue norther' hit would be damn near impossible. He could already feel a chill in the air. Dense, blue clouds were rolling in from the north. The temperature would drop twenty degrees in the next hour or two and they were probably close to three hours from the car.

Sydney unlaced her boot. Her face was tight with pain, her breath ragged. He eased the boot off her foot as gently as he could, but he could tell he was hurting her. When her foot was free, he peeled off the sock. Her ankle was swelling up fast, but at least there were no obvious bones sticking out.

"If we're lucky it's just a bad sprain," Russ said. "Have you ever broken anything before?"

"No. But this h-hurts bad."

"Put the sock back on for now. We need ice."

"Where can we find ice up here?" she asked as she gingerly pulled the sock over her swollen foot. "For that matter, how do we get back to the trail?"

He had ideas for both of those dilemmas. He helped her to stand, letting her lean on him as she balanced on one foot and brushed the leaves off her skirt. She was bleeding from a scrape on one knee, and the sleeve of her fake zebra jacket was torn almost all the way off, revealing a shredded silk blouse and another scrape on her shoulder.

He took off his backpack, stuffed her discarded boot inside and tossed the pack up the hill as far as he could. Then he stooped down, bracing his hands on his bent knees. "Climb aboard."

"What?"

"You're gonna ride piggyback. It's the only way I can think of to get you back to the trail. Hop on."

She was in no shape to argue. She did as he asked.

He wished she were pressing her body against him for some other reason. He was acutely aware of the feel of her bare thighs around his waist. Her tight skirt was probably hiked up as high as it would go. Her breasts were pressed against his back, her slender arms wrapped around his neck and her head was ear to ear with his. She'd lost her hat during her tumble down the hill, but he didn't remind her of it. The thing would just get in the way and he suspected it would be no use against freezing rain.

Climbing the steep hill with an extra hundred or so pounds on his back was no picnic, but he managed it, pulling himself up using saplings as handholds, being careful not to jar Sydney's injured foot in the process. Occasionally she made a quiet little gasp, and he knew the pain must be intense. But he had to hand it to her, she was pretty stoic. She ought to be cussing him up one side and down the other for getting her into this predicament.

This was what he got for trying to deceive her. He should have known better. Hell, he didn't want his old man's money because he hated the deceit and shallowness Sammy Oberlin represented. His money and his lifestyle had nearly ruined his and his mother's lives. When they'd moved to Linhart, they'd turned over a new leaf and started fresh, their lives based on honesty and integrity, the value of working for an honest living, being part of a community.

Yet he'd deceived Sydney in a big way. So much for honesty and integrity.

When he reached his backpack, he tossed it all the way up to the trail. A couple of minutes later he and Sydney made it safely to the trails themselves. He set Sydney down and caught his breath.

"How you doing?" he asked.

She shrugged, which probably meant not too well. Her ankle was the size of a softball inside her sock.

"Is there any way you can walk? Leaning on me for support and with a walking stick, maybe?"

She held on to his arm and tried to put weight on the foot. But there was no way. After three tiny steps she was in tears and her face was a stark white.

"Just leave me here to die," she said pathetically. "Save yourself."

"C'mon, gimpy. I can carry you." But her injury meant they wouldn't be returning to Linhart today, possibly not tomorrow, either. He could carry her three miles with no trouble—he often carried nearly that weight on long hiking trips. But he would have to move slowly on the rough trail to avoid another tumble, and they were running out of time. They'd spent too much time already. On the northern horizon, a wall of gray announced that the front was moving in—and it looked like a monster.

At least the cabin was stocked with plenty of provisions. Not gourmet fare, but they wouldn't starve.

Once she was securely on his back again, he started back up the trail.

"You're going the wrong way."

"We're going back to the cabin. It's too far to the car, and it's too dangerous trying to go downhill with you on my back."

"No, no, no, we have to get to town somehow. I need to get back home, I have work to do."

"Your work will have to wait."

"You don't understand. My aunt and my father will be worried about me."

"You're not exactly a kid," he pointed out. "I talked to your aunt yesterday and she didn't seem worried at all. Said she didn't need the car and to take your time, she would see you when she saw you."

"But my father…okay, maybe it's not that he's worried about me, it's the other way around. He's ill and I don't like leaving him alone."

"Ill?" Russ hadn't realized that. "What's wrong with him?"

"He had some health problems before my mother died, and then he went into something of a downward spiral, culminating in stomach surgery. Honestly, I thought he was going to starve himself to death. He's improving now, but he's a long way from self-sufficient."

Russ never would have done this to Sydney if he'd realized

she had a father back home who needed her. If anything happened to the man, it would be on Russ's conscience.

"I'm sorry, Sydney, really. But there's no way we can get back to town today. Unless…I could hike back alone and call in a medevac helicopter to fly you to a hospital. But the clearing at the cabin isn't big enough for a landing. We'd have to lower a line with a harness and raise you—"

"Stop, stop, you're making me dizzy. I don't like helicopters or hospitals and I definitely don't like the idea of dangling in the air. Besides, the way this wind is whipping up, I'm not sure a helicopter would work."

Russ had been thinking the same thing, but he'd been willing to try it if that was what she wanted.

"Your aunt promised she would call your father," he said, wanting to make her feel better about the situation. "She'll make sure he's okay."

Sydney grumbled a bit more, but there wasn't anything she could do.

When he reached the creek, he followed the steep trail down to the water's edge using a tree branch for support, then found a nice flat rock near where the water jumped over a little fall.

"How are we going to get across the creek?" Sydney asked as he eased her to the ground.

"One problem at a time. First, we're going to do the next best thing to icing up that ankle. This creek is spring-fed and it's freezing, even in summer."

Sydney folded her arms stubbornly even while balancing improbably on one foot. "I'm not sticking my foot in a freezing creek. It hurts badly enough as it is."

"Might take down the swelling, which would speed up your recovery," Russ pointed out. "The sooner your ankle's better, the sooner we can go home." He sat down on the rock, pulled out his pocketknife and started trimming his nails as if he had all the time in the world. He did it only because it was such a country-bumpkin thing to do that he knew it would infuriate her.

With a huff she leaned on his shoulder and maneuvered herself into a seated position next to him on the rock. She peeled off the sock. "Eww."

Her foot was turning blue. Not the best sign.

"How long do I have to leave it in the water?"

"About ten minutes should do it."

With another huff she plunged her foot into the water. "Yowwwww! Holy mackerel, son of a pigeon-toed sailor, that *hurts!*"

Russ winced. "Want me to tell you a story to take your mind off the pain?"

"No. I want you to reassure me I'm not going to lose all my toes to frostbite."

"Frostbite's not a threat in these temperatures," he said, though the cold north wind reminded him that hypothermia was. That lightweight jacket she had on was totally inadequate in anything below fifty degrees, and that temperature was rapidly approaching.

While she soaked her foot and called him bad names, Russ scouted along the creek until he found a better place to cross, rather than the log bridge they'd used before. He didn't want to try walking across the narrow log carrying Sydney on his back. But a little ways upstream the water was shallower and he could simply wade across. His boots would get wet, but they were only a few minutes from the cabin.

"It's been ten minutes," Sydney informed him when he returned. She already had her foot out of the water and was drying it off using her sock. She put the damp sock back on. "Can we go now?"

Even more colors were coming up on her ankle now: purple, red, green, black. They would be lucky if she could walk on it the next day. If not, he was going to have to hike out alone and bring help to transport Sydney off the mountain. He hoped the ice storm the weatherman had been talking about was only idle speculation. Those alarmist forecasts seldom came true.

With Sydney once again riding him like a horse, he started off to cover the last quarter-mile of the trail. "Does it feel any better?"

"It's cold," she groused.

When they reached the clearing and the cabin came into view, Sydney didn't try to disguise her sigh of relief. "And here I thought I never wanted to see this place again."

"Was it really that bad?"

"I had cold split-pea soup and sour canned cherries for lunch and I haven't bathed since yesterday morning. Yeah, it was bad."

"So you didn't know how to light the stove?" he asked.

"Maybe you grew up knowing how to start a fire with flint and corncobs, but I haven't a clue."

The poor thing. He'd meant to get her out of the way, not torture her.

*Oh, what a tangled web we weave...* He should have known better than to try to deceive anyone. It never worked. Even if he succeeded in sending Sydney back to New York ignorant of the fact he was Sammy Oberlin's son, what was to stop some other enterprising heir-finder from tracking him down the way Sydney had?

He should suck it up and tell her the truth. She was already mad at him. He would just have to make sure there were no knives or heavy, throwable objects within her reach when he told her he was going to refuse the inheritance.

## Chapter Eight

"Carry me to the bathroom," Sydney said the moment Russ brought her inside the cabin. "I'm taking a shower and no one is stopping me."

"You really should elevate that foot."

"I'm taking a shower," she said through gritted teeth. "I cannot stand being dirty one more instant."

The shower was actually a primitive tub conversion with a circular shower rod and a basic white plastic curtain. A tiny window let in just enough light to enable her to find the faucet. She reached inside the curtain and turned on the hot-water spigot. Nothing happened.

Russ hovered behind her, ready to catch her if she fell. "I'm afraid there's no hot water, only cold," Russ informed her.

"The nightmare continues." Sydney closed her eyes, then opened them, hoping to change reality. Still no hot water. She closed that faucet and turned on the cold, which rewarded her with a gush of rusty water that gradually turned clear. It wasn't just cold, it was icy.

She didn't care. She turned on the shower, then started unbuttoning her blouse. "Unless you want to see me naked, I suggest you leave."

He appeared to seriously consider the choice, which only made her madder. He'd blown any chances of seeing her naked when he'd tricked her into coming out to this nightmare of a cabin.

"Let me help you get your other shoe off," he said.

She was perfectly capable of doing that herself, but for some reason she let him help her. She sat on the edge of the tub while Russ unlaced her hiking boot. It felt sexy, having him remove an item of clothing, even if it was just a boot. She was ashamed to admit that riding on his back with her arms wrapped around him, she'd become even more aware of him as a man—his scent, the hardness of his muscles.

She didn't understand how she could be so angry and aroused at the same time, but there it was.

"I don't think my ankle's broken," she said. "It's starting to feel a little better." Whether this was the truth or merely wishful thinking, she didn't know.

"Good. I'll go turn on the generator, then bring you a robe."

It was the coldest shower Sydney had ever taken. It was also the fastest, unless she wanted to turn blue all over and catch pneumonia. The only soap in evidence was a small sliver in the soap dish. She used it gratefully.

When she turned off the water and opened the curtain, she found a towel and a flannel bathrobe hanging on a hook on the back of the door. With the towel in one hand she rubbed herself briskly, supporting herself on a towel bar with the other, still standing on only one leg. Her teeth were chattering as she wrapped the soft, flannel robe around her body.

She washed her underthings in the sink and hung them over a towel bar to dry. Now she could think about sitting down someplace and resting.

When she emerged from the bathroom, Russ raced to her side to help her to the ratty old sofa where she could stretch out and prop up her leg. Her ankle throbbed like nothing she'd ever felt before, and she'd known pain in her life. Though she'd only been five years old when she'd been attacked by the dog, she remembered the excruciating pain of her injuries and the subsequent surgeries as if they'd happened last week.

Though she got queasy at even the thought of entering a hospital, she wondered if she'd made the right decision in refusing the helicopter.

"Would you rather go to bed?" Russ asked.

Now, there was a loaded question. Her body responded as if he'd meant it in a different way. Considering her current opinion of him, her body needed to get with the program. "Um, no, the sofa. I'm not much of a lying-around-in-bed-person."

"Something tells me you're not much of a sitting-around-on-the-couch person, either." He set her down on the sofa, where she immediately stretched out.

"Why do you say that?"

"It didn't take me long to figure out that you're one of those people who can't sit still. Your schedule is always packed and you like to multitask. You work hard…and you play hard, but probably not often enough."

"Are you a psychic or something?" He'd nailed her. She was always trying to do two or three things at a time, always trying to squeeze one more client in, one more appointment early in the morning or in the evening. These past few months had been doubly hectic, tending to her father *and* his clients *and* his financial situation, keeping his house reasonably clean, cooking instead of eating out because her father missed her mom's cooking, not that Shirley had been any better at it than Sydney, who was an awful cook. She had let her leisure activities, what there were of them, slide because there simply wasn't time.

Russ laughed. "No, the signs are there for anyone to see. An unnatural attachment to your cell phone and restless hands. You fidget and drum your fingers and look at your watch a lot."

"Idle hands are the devil's tools," she quipped. "I happen to like getting things done."

He opened an old trunk and pulled out another crocheted afghan in a hideous green and orange zigzag pattern, to go with the granny-square blanket. He settled both blankets over her, then propped her swollen ankle on a pillow. "The blanket smells a little like mothballs, but I noticed you were shivering."

She wasn't surprised. The cabin had started to warm up earlier when the sun was shining through the windows. But now that the clouds had moved in, so had the chill.

Russ rubbed his hands together, obviously a bit chilled himself. "I'll get a fire started in here."

The fire sounded wonderful. And just a little too cozy. While Russ went outside to get extra wood, Sydney delved into her backpack where she'd stashed her purse and pulled out her pillbox. She always had Tylenol with her. Not that she ever got headaches, but she liked to be prepared for any eventuality. She swallowed a couple of caplets dry and hoped for the best.

What were they going to do stuck here until at least tomorrow? There was no television, no radio, no CD player. The only form of entertainment in evidence was a bookcase full of books. She supposed in a pinch she could wile away the hours by reading. Lord knew she didn't want to go back anywhere near those boxes of papers in the loft. She'd seen enough of Bert Klausen's family to last a lifetime.

When Russ returned he had an armload of firewood for the stove. It looked like enough to keep them warm for a while. She watched with interest as he went about the business of building a fire.

"My gosh, what did you do in here?" He scratched his head as he stared into the pile of matches she'd left on top of the logs she'd loaded into the stove.

"What does it look like? I tried to light a fire."

"You can't just light logs with a match. You need kindling and starter material—"

"Well, I didn't know that! How do you do it?"

"You need small sticks first." He selected a few about the width of his finger and arranged them in a loose pile. "Then you need something to get the fire started. Newspaper will do." There was, indeed, a stack of yellowed newspapers against the wall near the stove. He took a section, separated the pages and wrinkled one of them up, positioning it strategically in the pile of sticks, then grabbed the box of matches.

When he opened the box, a puzzled look crossed his face. "How many did you use?"

"A bunch."

"Well, let's hope I'm better at this than you are, or we're in for a cold night."

She didn't think she could stand another night freezing her butt off. Hmm. Maybe they'd have to snuggle together to conserve body warmth. Oh, hell, where had that thought come from? She was supposed to be mad at him.

He only took one match to do the job. In moments a cheerful blaze was burning inside the stove. Russ began feeding in larger sticks and logs. He watched it, occasionally poking it with a metal stick, until he was satisfied that the thing wasn't going to fizzle out. Finally he closed the grate.

*Manly man makes fire.* He was building heat in other places besides the stove. Apparently Sydney's hormones were not indifferent to the fire-building or the whole rescuing the damsel in distress. What next? Would he go out in the forest and bring home a woolly mammoth? And if he did, would she throw herself at him in a fit of abject feminine adoration? Why did this Daniel Boone stuff make him so appealing?

It was the novelty of it all, she decided. She didn't know many men in New York who could survive away from Manhattan for longer than a few hours. Some she knew would positively wither away without their daily Starbucks and *New York Times* crossword puzzle.

Russ sat in the big easy chair across from Sydney. "So what was it like, growing up in New York? Did you have a big family?"

"No, I'm an only. And it wasn't like I was raised in a skyscraper. We had a little house in Brooklyn—my father still lives there. I went to public school and did all the normal things."

"I take it you were very close to your parents."

"In a way. Truthfully, they were always so wrapped up in each other and the business that they never paid that much attention to me, so long as I stayed out of trouble. But I was okay with that. I didn't want them to dote on me the way my friends' parents seemed to. I was always off doing my own thing, anyway. If there can be an upside to my mom's death, it's that my dad and I have grown closer. I know him better now than I ever have."

"You followed in their footsteps, so there must have been some fondness there."

Sydney laughed. "Probably I became a private investigator because I wanted to prove something to them. That I was as good as they were, something like that. But I found out I really did like the work. So it's all turned out okay.

"What was it like for *you,* growing up here? You did grow up here, didn't you?" she qualified, remembering that Russ didn't have that strong Texas drawl common among Linhart's residents.

He looked wary for a moment, but then it seemed to pass. She remembered then that he'd never had a father. Maybe things hadn't been so sunny, growing up illegitimate in a small town.

"I don't have any siblings, either," he said. "We lived with my grandmother for a time, but mostly it's been just Mom and me. She always made everything an adventure. She was like a kid herself, sometimes. Then there was Bert—he kind of unofficially adopted me. He's the one who taught me all the outdoors stuff."

"So while I was running wild on the sidewalks of New York, you were running wild in the countryside."

"Pretty much. Linhart is a good place for a kid. Everybody knows everybody and we all watch out for each other."

They fell silent for a while. Sydney stared up at the timber ceiling. "Who built this cabin?"

"Bert's grandfather, or maybe great-grandfather, Victor Klausen."

"Wouldn't that make him your great-grandfather, too?" Sydney asked. "Since you two are cousins and all."

"I'm related on his mother's side. We're only distant cousins."

"So you knew all along I wouldn't find anything about the Kleins here."

"I really didn't know what all was here," he said uneasily.

"You're really not a very good liar. But right now, I'm going to choose not to pursue the reasons why you worked so hard to get rid of me. You're stuck with me now, pal."

"It's not that big of a hardship."

There he was, flirting again. "So, about the cabin. How old is it?"

"At least a hundred years. It was all done by hand. Can you imagine cutting those trees down with a hand saw, working each log, fitting them together so exactly? You don't see that kind of craftsmanship anymore. I'm trying to keep the place in good repair for Bert. He doesn't come up here often anymore."

Sydney imagined the hike would be a bit rigorous for a man Bert's age. If he came here at all, it was testament to his health.

She leaned back against the pillows and closed her eyes, thinking she'd rest just for a moment.

The next thing she knew, it was dark outside and a wonderful smell was drifting through the cabin. Her ankle had awakened her; apparently the Tylenol had worn off.

She sat up and rubbed her eyes. That was when she realized Russ had tucked the afghan around her and added a third blanket, a solid-blue woolly thing. But the cabin was also toasty warm and Russ was bustling around working at something on the cook top of the woodstove, the source of the heavenly smell.

A man who could cook. Surely whatever he'd concocted wasn't out of a can. The closest thing to a man who could cook among her New York friends was one who could get them dinner reservations at the latest trendy restaurant.

She found her purse and a couple more painkillers. Something stronger would have been welcome, but the over-the-counter stuff at least took the edge off her discomfort.

She chanced a look at her ankle. The swelling had gone down some, but the Technicolor special effects were even more dramatic. She'd never seen such creative bruising.

"You're awake," Russ said.

"Mmm. Sorry I passed out on you like that. You must have been bored, sitting around with no one to talk to."

"I'm never bored up here. There's always something to do—hiking, fishing or just sitting outside listening to the wind in the trees. Even when the weather's bad, like today, there are always repairs and improvements to make on the cabin. Just keeping it clean takes time. The place gets dusty even when no one is here."

Even better. A man who wasn't afraid of a little housework. More and more she was beginning to see that Russ was a breed apart.

"What are you cooking?"

"Fried potatoes with onion."

"That's what we're having for dinner?" Not that she was complaining. After her previous few meals, just about anything sounded insanely delicious.

"I'll heat up some chili, too."

"Where did the potatoes and onions come from?"

"There were a few Idahos in the bin under the counter. They keep a pretty long time in the cool and dark. The onions I picked earlier today, on the way up here. They're wild onions, growing along the side of the trail, and I figured the freeze would kill them so I might as well harvest a few." He flipped the potatoes with the skill of someone who knew how to use a skillet and spatula.

"We can have canned fruit for dessert," he continued. "Pineapples or peaches, your choice."

"Wait a minute. How can you tell what's in the cans? The labels are missing."

"The contents are written on the bottoms with a Magic Marker. We had a flood at the store that washed the labels off a few cases of canned goods. We were able to identify the cans by the cartons, but we couldn't sell them. So we bring them up here or eat them at home."

"You might have told me to look on the bottoms of the cans," she huffed. "You wouldn't believe the nauseating meals I ate—cold."

Russ laughed, but then quickly sobered. "I'm sorry. I should have taken more time to prepare you for an overnight stay here. I had no idea you wouldn't know how to light the stove. It's pretty much like a fireplace or a campfire."

"My fireplace at home is electric and I've never been camping in my life."

"Never? Not even on a Girl Guide overnight?"

"Never."

"That is the saddest case I've ever heard."

"Have you ever been to Macy's during a clearance sale?"

"What? No. What does that have to do with anything?"

"That is the saddest thing *I've* ever heard. Our lifestyles are different. That doesn't mean yours is better than mine. I happen to prefer bricks and concrete to trees and dirt."

"Touché." He flipped the potatoes onto a plate, then set about heating up the chili. She noticed he opened the can a lot more easily than she had.

"I just don't understand why people would deliberately make themselves uncomfortable," she said. "Hike up a mountain into the godforsaken boonies so they can sit in a tiny cabin with no central heat and air, no TV, no phone and substandard food."

"And I don't understand why people would choose to commute through hours of rush-hour traffic, breathe polluted air and never have a moment's silence."

Okay, maybe he had a point. Although she walked when she could, her job required that she spend a lot of time in her car, cursing the traffic, the smell of car exhaust and the noise.

"I guess we'll just have to agree to disagree about this," she said.

"Fine with me," he said amiably, but with the attitude of someone who secretly knew he was right.

When the chili was hot, Russ poured it into thick ceramic bowls. "Do you want to eat at the table or should I rig up a tray for you?"

"I can come to the table," she said, not wanting to be treated like an invalid.

After he'd set their dinner and some dishes on the rough plank table, Russ helped Sydney to one of the ladder-back chairs. She still couldn't put any weight on her left foot, but using a carved walking stick Russ had found and leaning heavily on him, she managed. Russ brought a small pillow from the sofa and propped her leg up on a second chair.

"You're being so nice," she said. "I feel really foolish, injuring myself and forcing you to be stranded with me, cooking for me…"

"It's no big deal," he said gruffly. "I told you I like spending time up here and Bert can handle the store for a couple of days. It's not like I have many clients this time of year."

"What about the dog?"

"Bert will take care of Nero, too."

"Well, this smells really good." She took a bite of the chili.

It was pretty tasty—she'd always liked chili, even the kind that came out of a can.

"Okay for substandard fare? Not too hot?"

"I didn't mean *this* was substandard," she said, wishing she hadn't been so critical of this place earlier. "I was referring to the other meals I ate here. This is good chili, nice and spicy."

"That's one thing we have in common. I love spicy food, the hotter the better."

"Well, you'd be a mighty strange Texan if you didn't like hot food. Aren't you native Texans born with hot sauce running through your veins instead of normal blood?"

"Oh, but I wasn't born in Texas. I spent the first—" He abruptly cut himself off, the look of panic in his eyes unmistakable.

Russ COULD NOT BELIEVE he'd made such a hideous blunder. But subterfuge didn't come easily to him. Sydney was right that he was a bad liar. He was just too damn honest for his own good. Of course, he'd decided it would be better to tell her the truth. But deciding and actually doing it were two different things. He'd wanted to pick the time.

"Where were you born?" Sydney asked innocently.

"Um…" Until now, he'd consoled himself with the fact he hadn't lied outright to her. But now he was either going to have to lie or she would know he was the Russ Klein she was looking for.

"Russ? Cat got your tongue?"

"Let's just say I'm not a native Texan. But my mom's family is from Texas—right here in the Hill Country."

"And you moved back here to be closer to them?"

"Yeah."

"Where did you move from? I have noticed you don't talk like a Texan."

Hell. He was sunk. Even if he lied, she would probably know he was lying, which would only make things worse. He felt guilty enough about luring her up to this cabin under false pretenses and letting her injure herself. If he didn't come clean now, he'd dig his hole even deeper—not that he wasn't already so deep he'd need an elevator to get out of it.

"Russ, are you going to tell me where you were born?"

He blew out a breath, resigned. "Nevada."

"Las Vegas?"

"Yes."

"Was your father Sammy Oberlin?"

"Unfortunately, yes."

Sydney went very still. "Oh, my God. Oh, my God, you're him, you're really him. I knew my instincts were right about you." Then she paused, staring at him with an uncomprehending look on her face. "Why did you lie to me?"

## Chapter Nine

"I didn't exactly lie," he tried, but she was having none of it.

"You *knew* I was looking for you and you did everything in your power to convince me I was on the wrong track, including letting me waste two days hiking up to this godforsaken place—"

"I know, I know. I shouldn't have done it. But if you'd stayed in Linhart you eventually would've met someone who knew the truth. I had to find a way to get you out of town."

"You could've sent me on a wild-goose chase somewhere besides here," she said. "Maybe to a spa, or a resort."

"This was the first thing I thought of. I figured all the papers and letters and pictures upstairs would keep you busy."

"But not forever. Or were you planning for me not to come back…ever?"

He hoped she was kidding. "I was going to send my mother to the spa, actually. But that didn't work out like I planned." His mother had simply called the spa and rescheduled her visit for next month, easy as pie.

He braced himself for Sydney's explosion. Whatever she threw at him, he deserved it. If he ended up without the chili pot over his head, he'd be lucky.

But the explosion never came. She was studying him as if he were some new species of insect she'd never seen before.

"I really don't understand. I've seen people lie, cheat and steal to try to inherit money that didn't belong to them. But I've never seen anyone work this hard *not* to inherit money."

"It's complicated."

"Enlighten me."

"I don't want to be rich. I've seen what extreme wealth can do to people. How much do you know about my father?"

"Sammy? Not a whole lot, other than that he owned a very profitable casino and had ties to organized crime. That part isn't my business. His will is my business. He left you half of his estate—he must have loved you a great deal."

Russ laughed. "You gotta be kidding."

"Well, something caused him to write his will that way."

"Maybe he wanted to get revenge on his wife by cutting her out of her inheritance."

"She received more than ten million, as well, so it wasn't that."

"Then the gesture was born out of pure guilt." That was the only thing Russ could figure.

"Who cares why he did it? He did— it's ten million dollars. You can't just pretend it doesn't exist."

"That's exactly what I have in mind. The poor bastard thought anything could be bought or sold with cold hard cash. Well, not me. He can't buy my forgiveness for what he did, not with any amount."

Sydney was silent for a while. She ate some of the potatoes, chewing thoughtfully. "What did he do that was so horrible? Did he abuse you?"

"Maybe I could have dealt with that. What he did was almost worse. To Sammy Oberlin, I was invisible. I didn't exist.

He wanted my mother in his bed, but he certainly didn't want to marry her or take any responsibility for the consequences."

"He didn't pay child support?"

"He always handed my mother money for whatever she claimed she needed, but there were never any formal payments."

"So this whole thing is a gesture of defiance," Sydney concluded. "A grudge match between you and your deceased father. Who do you think is winning?"

When she put it like that, it sounded ridiculous. "There's more to it."

"So keep explaining."

"I don't owe you an explanation. My reasons are my own. Let's just leave it at that."

She sat there silently for a while, pondering. "All right," she finally said. "If you'll help me carry the dishes to the sink, I'll wash them."

"You don't have to—"

"You cooked, it's only fair I clean."

He had to give her credit, she was trying to honor his wishes. But try as she might, it was clear she was confused and upset by his decision. He supposed he couldn't blame her. No one liked being duped. "I'm sorry I can't be more accommodating."

She shrugged. "It's just a million-dollar commission. Easy come, easy go. You brought me up to this cabin under false pretenses. I almost froze to death, I had to use that disgusting outhouse because you neglected to tell me there was a marginally adequate bathroom, I ate the grossest meals imaginable because you didn't tell me the can labels were on the bottom, but, hey, you don't owe me anything. And I'm not the kind of person to carry a grudge." She managed to get herself upright and hobble to the kitchen sink without his assistance.

"Just bring me the dishes, okay? I can lean against the counter. It's probably best if we don't talk about this anymore."

She was probably afraid she'd do him violence if they talked any more. They were stuck with each other and isolated from any witnesses.

Russ decided he better do as she asked and consider himself lucky she wasn't throwing dishes instead of washing them.

He carried their dishes to the sink and saw that Sydney was staring at the pump, mystified. Good gravy, she didn't know how to work a pump, either?

"If the bathroom has running water," she asked, "why doesn't the kitchen?"

"Because Bert did exactly what was needed to put in a bathroom. No more, no less. The pump worked fine, so why replace it?"

"So idiots like me can wash dishes?"

Russ put a large pot in the sink. She stood aside and let him pump away, and after thirty or so seconds, a stream of cold water started to fill the pot. "I'll have to heat some water on the stove. You might want to take a seat."

Sydney scraped their plates into the trash, then hopped back to the table and sat with her chin propped on one hand while Russ heated the water. He tried to think of something to say, some avenue of conversation that wouldn't start them arguing. But he couldn't think of anything.

When the water was warm enough, he dumped it into a dishpan with some dish soap and Sydney began washing the dishes without a word, handing them to him when they were clean. He rinsed in cold, then dried and stacked. The silence was anything but companionable.

"I'm sorry," he said. "I told you it was complicated."

"You could do a lot of good things with that money," she said, not sounding quite as tense as before. Maybe the act of washing dishes had soothed her—the warm water, the scent of the lemon dish soap. He'd never minded washing dishes for that reason.

"So instead of the rich guy, I'd be the idiot who gave away ten million dollars. The press would love that." Not to mention his mother would never speak to him again.

"You could start a charitable foundation," she tried again.

"That's a nice thought, but there's no way. Admit it. If I accepted that money, my life would be changed forever. I happen to like my life just as it is."

"I think that's selfish."

"What? I'm selfish because I won't accept ten million dollars?"

"How do you know being rich would change your life for the worse? Have you ever been rich before?"

"In a matter of speaking, yes. When my mother was Sammy Oberlin's common-law wife, we had everything money could buy and it was the most miserable existence you can imagine. Throwing money at people doesn't solve problems, it creates them."

"Speak for yourself," she said curtly. Then she sighed. "I told you we shouldn't talk about this anymore. I'm tired and cranky and my ankle hurts, so I'm going to bed. By tomorrow I'm sure my ankle will feel better. I want to get up first thing in the morning and start back. I don't care if I have to hop all the way or crawl. I'll get there somehow." With that she dumped the dirty dishwater down the sink, grabbed her walking stick and limped toward the bedroom.

She closed the door with a firm, decisive snick, which was

a pretty good indication that she didn't want his company, not that that was even a remote possibility.

It was way too early to go to bed. Russ added another log to the fire, noticing for the first time that the cabin was getting colder despite the fact the stove had been burning hot for several hours. He checked the thermometer that hung just outside one of the windows, shining a flashlight on it from inside.

Holy cow, it was already below freezing. He knew one thing, the bedroom would be the coldest room in the house. If Sydney insisted on keeping that door closed, she might be nothing more than a Sydney-cicle by morning.

Knowing the reception wouldn't be too welcoming, he went to the bedroom and tapped on the door. When he got no answer, he tapped a little harder.

"Sydney? I know you don't want to speak to me ever again and I don't blame you, but you're going to freeze if you don't open the door to let some warm air in."

No answer.

He opened the door a crack and peered in. Sydney was asleep in the exact middle of the old iron-framed double bed, rolled up in a little ball with the quilt wrapped around her. Only her nose and a bit of her hair were visible.

Poor thing, she was probably already blue from the cold. The wind outside was howling and the log cabin was designed for Texas summers, not frozen winters. He could actually feel cold air gusting through the single-pane windows.

He did the only charitable thing. He walked to the bed, scooped her up in his arms and carried her into the main room.

She stirred as he laid her on the couch. "What are you doing?" she asked muzzily, not quite awake.

"I'm putting you near the fire to warm you up."

She surprised him by throwing her arms around his neck. "Mmm, I could think of better ways to warm me up."

Whoa. She had to be asleep—probably thought he was some other guy, some lover she had back in New York. But that didn't stop his body from responding. He was instantly hard, and the idea of sliding in beside her on the couch and bundling up with her under a mound of blankets got stuck in his mind and wouldn't leave.

But he'd abused the poor woman enough. He wouldn't add seducing her when she was asleep to his list of sins. He gently disentangled her arms from his neck.

"Not tonight, sleepyhead."

She was already in dreamland, probably unaware of his words.

Unable to resist, he touched his lips to hers.

She might be sleeping, but she still responded and he allowed it for three glorious seconds before he made himself pull away.

The woman was a bundle of contradictions. She represented all the things he'd left behind in Las Vegas—a slick city woman with an unhealthy fascination with other people's money. If anything, she was an even worse match for him than Deirdre or Melanie or the others. At least they'd lived within driving distance.

But she loved her father, that much was certain. She'd put her own career on hold to help him out after her mother's death. And she'd been a pretty good sport about getting stuck out here in the boonies—well, until he'd gone and blurted out the whole story.

Damn him and his big mouth. Although, he had to say, he felt better now that the lie was off his chest.

He dragged the sofa closer to the stove. If Sydney was determined to start for town tomorrow morning—and he didn't doubt for a minute that she was—he was at least going to ensure she got a good night's sleep.

SYDNEY AWOKE, disoriented at first by her lumpy bed and the smell of wood smoke. But then she saw the glow of the dying fire and she realized the cold had awakened her.

How had she gotten to the sofa?

Russ, of course. He'd carried her out here to be closer to the fire. She didn't know whether to be miffed that he'd violated her privacy or grateful he'd been worried about her comfort.

Gratitude won out.

Maybe she should put another log on the fire. Her walking stick was still in the bedroom, but she could hop that far.

She flung off her blankets, bracing herself for the cold air, glad she'd taken the time to change into a pair of sweatpants and another flannel shirt. They might not be flattering, but they were warm.

She pushed up on her good leg and steadied herself, took one hop and promptly tripped over something.

"What the hell!"

"Ow!"

Sydney caught herself and rolled to the side, preventing yet another calamitous injury. "Russ, is that you?"

"Who else would it be?"

"I'm so sorry," she said automatically. "I never saw you there. Did I hurt you?"

He sat up. "No, you just scared the bejeezus out of me." She knew he was lying, though, because he was rubbing his head.

"What are you doing sleeping on the floor?"

"Staying warm. What are you doing wandering around in a dark room?"

"I was going to put another log on the fire."

"Let me do it." He helped her back to the sofa, where she gladly climbed back under her layer of blankets—four of them, she realized.

"You carried me in here?"

"It's in the twenties outside. You were going to freeze in the bedroom."

"Thank you."

"You're welcome," he said gruffly.

"Listen, about how I acted earlier—I'm really sorry. You have every right to refuse your inheritance. I was just frustrated, that's all. Locating the Oberlin heir—it's like the holy grail for someone in the heir-finding business. We've all taken a crack at it. There's a whole Web site dedicated to you, did you know that?"

He poked at the fire. "I had no idea. What will they do with the money if the heir can't be found?"

"There's no statute of limitations. You or your heirs can claim it at any time."

"I guess that kind of money does draw public attention. You could retire on the commission alone."

"Some people could."

Russ gave the fire a few more pokes, leaving the grate open so the room would warm up faster. Then he crawled back under his own blankets. He'd made a pallet on the floor next to the couch. Good thing this place had plenty of blankets.

"How much money would *you* need to retire?" he asked. "Or would no amount be enough?"

"Number one, I'm not interested in retiring. I love my work. Number two, if I earned a million-dollar commission, I would put it to use, never fear."

"Doing what? Buying clothes?"

"Yeah. Clothes, jewelry, trips to Paris," she said flippantly. "That's all women are interested in, right?"

She turned over, facing the back of the sofa, indicating the conversation was closed. Damn it, she'd been prepared to give him the benefit of the doubt. But when he blithely assumed she wanted the commission simply because she was greedy, she could have smacked him and enjoyed it. Her plans for that money were none of his business. Just like his reasons for refusing the inheritance were none of hers.

"I'm sorry," he said softly. "That was rude. I don't know enough about you to make assumptions about your motives."

She would have continued the argument, but her throat was closed up, her eyes burning and she didn't want him to know how close to the breaking point she was. But Baines & Baines was on the brink of financial collapse, and the strain of juggling bills and making excuses to bill collectors had taken its toll on her. Unless her father performed some major financial miracle, Sydney was going to have to look into Chapter 11 as soon as she returned to New York. She'd taken a gamble, spending the last of her ready funds to follow a hunch on this disaster of a business trip, and she'd lost. Her hunch had been right and still she'd lost.

She felt a hand on her shoulder.

"What?"

"I'm sorry," he said again.

"Yeah, I got that." They seemed to be spending a lot of their time being rude and then apologizing to each other.

"I have a question. Did Sammy Oberlin actually name me, specifically, in his will?"

"Yes, he did. 'My son, Russell.' Unfortunately, he neglected to mention your last name."

"And Paula, his wife, got the other half."

"Yes."

Sydney closed her eyes, thinking the conversation was over. But just as she was about to drift off, Russ spoke again. "I still can't believe he did that. He was a rotten father. I saw him when he would pick up my mother to take her to a party or whatever, but he wanted nothing to do with me. Sometimes he bought me elaborate presents for birthdays and Christmas, but that was mostly to keep my mother happy."

"Maybe he just didn't know how to relate to kids," Sydney said, drawn into the conversation despite her intention to never speak to Russ again. "Some people are afraid of kids. And it might appear they don't like children, but it might be they just don't know how to behave around them."

Russ actually chuckled. "Kind of like you and dogs."

"I'm not afraid of dogs," came her instant denial.

"Uh-huh. So you think my old man left me ten million bucks because that was the only way he knew how to relate to me? Through money?"

"It seems a logical explanation to me. You said he bought you expensive presents when you were a child."

"He paid my mother off to be rid of us. He wanted to marry Paula, but she wouldn't tie the knot unless Winnie and I were out of his life forever. She didn't want the possibility of a pretty, pseudo-ex-wife turning Sammy's head and she sure didn't want any of his time or attention diverted by a kid that wasn't hers. So Sammy paid off my mom to legally sever his parental ties to me and move out of state. Those aren't the actions of someone who gives a damn."

"Hormones will make a man do crazy things," Sydney pointed out. "Men do all kinds of insane things in the name of love. Women, too."

"I'm not buying it. You know what I think?"

"No, but you're going to tell me."

"It's like I said before—I think he did it out of spite. He probably found out after a while that marriage to Paula wasn't all sweetness and light. Hell, I could have told him that. And he knew leaving money to me would make her crazy. She knew exactly who I was, but she never mentioned it, did she?"

"No. She claimed she didn't know he had a son."

"Doesn't surprise me."

"So you know Paula?"

"She was another showgirl, like my mom. She was actually a friend of Mom's. Supposedly. But anyone with half a brain could see Paula was after Sammy from the very beginning. Mom refused to believe it. She was incredibly naive. Still is."

Sydney turned to face him, giving up on the notion of sleep. She found Russ lying on his back close to the sofa, his hands clasped behind his head, the fire illuminating his strong profile and making his sun-bleached highlights glow. Her heart stumbled just looking at him, his face so unguarded as he stared up at the ceiling, lost in memory.

"Well," she said, "we may never know Sammy's motives. So that's why you won't take the money? To spite your father? Trust me, he won't know the difference."

"No, that's not why I don't want the money." He rolled over to his side, his back to her. Apparently the subject was closed. Again.

Fine. She flopped over onto her stomach and let out a sharp yelp when she jostled her ankle, having forgotten about it.

"What?"

"Nothing," she said quickly. "I bumped my foot. Go to sleep."

"Yes, ma'am."

The cabin was quiet—unnaturally so. The wind had died down and, unlike the previous night, no animals shrieked or croaked or rustled or scratched. They'd all burrowed somewhere warm for the night, no doubt. All Sydney could hear was the occasional crackle of the fire, the whisper of the ashes shifting and Russ's soft breathing.

She couldn't sleep. It was so still it was creepy. How did anyone sleep without the comforting noise of traffic, sirens and the pounding of a base beat every few minutes as a car with a killer stereo drove past the building?

Then she noticed a different noise, and this one she did know—a clicking patter against the window.

Freezing rain. Falling ice. Whatever you wanted to call it, it wasn't supposed to fall in central Texas, not even in January.

She cursed her luck. Hopping down the mountain she could have managed; ice she could have dealt with. But not both at the same time. She wasn't going to make it out of these woods tomorrow.

# Chapter Ten

Sydney must have fallen back to sleep, because the next thing she was aware of, the light of dawn poured through the windows bathing everything in an orange-pink glow and Russ was shaking her shoulder.

Well, not shaking, exactly. He was rubbing her arm lightly, his touch warm and sensuous. Her body tingled all over and in the fuzzy world between waking and sleeping, Sydney's natural guard was down. She snuggled deeper under the down quilt and enjoyed the purely physical sensations.

"Sydney?"

"Hmm?"

"You awake?"

"I am now." Gradually she dragged herself out of the sensual haze as she remembered where she was and with whom.

Oh, dear. Somehow Russ had made her feel all sexy and he hadn't even been trying. He'd probably just wanted her to wake up.

She rolled over, finding his face too close to hers for comfort. "Is something wrong?" But she could tell just by looking at his face that nothing was wrong. He wore the expression of a kid on Christmas morning.

"No, nothing's wrong. And I'm sorry for waking you. But yesterday you asked me how anyone could stand to live in the middle of nowhere—"

"I think I referred to it as the godforsaken boonies," she corrected him.

"Well, I have an answer for you. But you have to get up to see it."

"See what?"

He all but dragged her to her feet, or rather foot, because she still couldn't put weight on her left ankle.

"Where's my walking stick?"

"Never mind, just lean on me. You're gonna miss it."

"Miss what?"

He didn't answer. He just led her toward the big picture window that looked out onto the woods, a window she truthfully hadn't paid much attention to before because the novelty of staring at winter-dead trees had worn off. But when she looked out, her breath caught in her throat.

The scene before her was a fairyland of glistening, sparkling ice, all tinted the most incredible shade of pink as the sun struggled to mount the horizon. Each branch, each leaf, each blade of grass was encased in a thin sheet of ice.

Into the midst of this wonderland, two deer calmly pawed at the ground and nibbled blades of winter grass uncovered by their sharp hooves. They were so close, Sydney could see the individual hairs that made up their coats.

"Oh!" was all she could think to say. She was literally struck dumb by the sheer beauty and she felt a ridiculous urge to cry. She'd never before truly understood the meaning of *awe inspiring*.

"This is why I come up here," Russ said softly. She was

still leaning on him to steady herself and it seemed perfectly natural when he slipped an arm around her shoulders.

Something startled the deer and they bounded off into the woods, white tails flashing. But Russ and Sydney continued to watch in companionable silence as the panorama changed with the rising sun, pink and orange gradually giving way to the bright sun and a flawless blue sky. An owl floated by on its way home from a long night of foraging and a couple of squirrels poked their heads out of one of the trees after it had passed.

"Thank you for sharing that with me," Sydney said. "It'll be my fondest memory of my visit to the Hill Country."

"And here I thought *I* would be your fondest memory."

She looked up at him to find his eyes dancing with laughter and she felt an inexplicable urge to kiss him. A heartbeat later his expression fell serious and she realized he must have somehow read her mind, or she'd read his, because he was leaning in. She closed her eyes and let it happen. What was the harm?

As his mouth captured hers, a feeling of warmth stole across her senses and she ceased to notice the chilly cabin. The blanket she'd wrapped around her shoulders dropped and her arms went around his neck.

The kiss felt familiar, as if she'd dreamed it many times, and her dream lover had suddenly become flesh and blood, known to her in some instinctual way.

Russ moved his hand up the back of her flannel shirt, his touch sending tremors of desire shooting through her. Suddenly she ached for his touch everywhere and probably wouldn't have objected if he'd taken the kiss further. But too soon, he pulled back, placing one final, light kiss on her forehead and then just holding her.

"I have a confession," he said. "Last night, when I carried you out from the bedroom, I kissed you."

She pulled back and looked up at him, not sure she believed him. How could she sleep through a kiss from this man? "You kissed a defenseless, sleeping woman?"

"You were only sort of asleep. You, um, must have thought I was someone else."

Her face warmed as she wondered what, exactly, she'd said or done. She'd been told that she talked in her sleep. She decided not to press him for details—too embarrassing. "You didn't have to tell. You could've gotten away with it," she said as they made their way back to the sofa. Standing on one leg was tiring, even when she was getting the stuffing kissed out of her.

"I'm compulsively honest. As I made painfully clear last night, I suck at lying. When I was a teenager, if I came in past curfew, I always woke up my mom and confessed. I never should have tried to mislead you. I'm not good at that sort of thing."

"Don't apologize for being too honest. Honesty is an admirable quality," Sydney said, meaning it. Not that there would be much work for a private investigator if people always told the truth.

"I thought you didn't have ice and snow this far south," Sydney said, still gazing at the icy panorama from her spot on the sofa.

"It's rare, but not unheard of. We get an ice storm or a dusting of snow every few years."

"We won't be hiking back today," she said glumly, though surprisingly the idea didn't alarm her as much as it would have yesterday. This cabin was far more appealing now that she had decent food, running water and a source of heat.

"I'm glad to hear you say that. If you'd held firm on your

threat to make it back to town today, I'd have felt compelled to hike after you and probably would have ended up carrying you back here again."

His razzing almost made her want to give it a try. There were worse things in this world than riding Russ Klein.

WINNIE STOOD at the window of her beauty salon, looking out onto Main Street. They'd hardly had any customers today because of the weather. Quite a few had canceled, and others simply hadn't shown up.

The ice was starting to melt now, so the street was passable. The afternoon would probably pick up, she told herself, not that business was ever a problem at the Cut 'n' Curl. She was the best hairdresser in town. Well, okay, she owned the only salon in town unless you counted Wick's Barber Shop. The lack of business wasn't what troubled her. It was the fact that Russ hadn't come home yesterday from wherever he'd gone so suddenly.

He'd gone for a hike—that's what he'd told Bert. And he simply hadn't come back.

"No sign of Russ yet, huh?" asked Betty, Winnie's best friend since kindergarten. The two had lost touch during Winnie's Las Vegas years, but when Winnie moved back to her hometown to live with her mother—after she'd blown most of her money—she and Betty had taken up like there'd never been a lapse. It was Betty who'd suggested Winnie ought to buy the Cut 'n' Curl and get her cosmetology license.

"No, haven't seen him yet," Winnie said.

"I'm sure he's fine, hon. You know Russ, he goes his own way."

"I'm sure he's fine, too." But the thing that really bothered

Winnie was that white car parked smack in front of the general store. Winnie suspected Russ and the city girl were together somewhere. And that troubled her. Especially since Russ had been so obviously secretive about why the woman had come to Linhart. He'd been hiding something from her—she was sure of it.

Winnie knew of one person who probably had the answer. Bert Klausen was a dear friend, the father and grandfather Russ had never had. If Russ had turned out well, Winnie knew it wasn't due to her influence. She'd been a careless mother, not exactly neglectful, just consumed with her own problems and dramas. Russ had always been so good, so well behaved, that she hadn't given him a whole lot of extended, concentrated thought and attention in his early years.

Bert was the one who'd taken the boy fishing, shown him how to do all that wilderness stuff, even how to do his income taxes, and Russ had eaten it up with a spoon. Bert had always been there for them. He was widowed, his children grown and moved away, so the Kleins and Bert had been a good fit.

"Betty, hold the fort for a little while, will you? I'm going to run over to the store and pick up a couple of things for dinner."

Winnie put on her good winter coat, which she'd happily dug out from the back of the closet that morning. Not much call for a heavy coat here, but hers was nice, a real camel hair with classic styling that Russ had given her for Christmas a few years back. She slipped it on, pulled on a pair of gloves and stepped out into the chilly air.

Her high heels were useless for winter weather, but some thoughtful soul had sanded the sidewalks and street, so Winnie was able to mince her way carefully down one block and across the street to the general store. The bell over the door rang as she entered, and Bert, sitting in his usual place reading his newspaper, looked up with a smile.

"Well, hello, there, Winnie," he said. "Cold enough for you?"

"Oh, I love the cold weather, even if it is bad for business," she said. "It's such a rarity. Wish we'd have a real snow, though, instead of this ice."

"Got snow up in Dallas," he said. Bert loved talking about the weather.

"I just need to pick up a couple of cans of chicken stock," she said. "Oh, by the way, you haven't heard from Russ, have you?"

"Not a peep," Bert said as he pushed himself out of his rocking chair and walked over to the shelves where he kept the canned goods. "But don't you worry, Russ can take care of himself. He's probably holed up at the cabin."

"What about the woman with the white car?" Winnie asked as casually as she could. "I think her name is Sydney. Any sign of her?"

"What woman?" Bert said with obviously feigned ignorance.

"Bert, I just told you what woman. The one with the white beemer that's parked right in front of the store."

"Oh, that woman. Nope, nope, haven't seen her."

"Okay, Bert, what do you know that I don't know? Is she Russ's new girlfriend?" Russ's story that Sydney was some kind of stalker had sounded fishy to her. Normally Russ didn't lie to her, but he would if he thought he needed to protect her somehow.

It wouldn't surprise her if Sydney had caught Russ's eye. He had a habit of taking up with beautiful, sophisticated women, and in theory Winnie had no trouble with that. But they never worked out in the long run. They were always nice enough girls. Winnie was even a little jealous of them some-times, with their designer clothes and their exciting city jobs. But she knew enough about Russ that that sort of girl wouldn't make a good wife for him.

"I never heard him speak of her before," Bert said.

"But you know something about her I don't," Winnie said.

"Now, what would I know? I just sit here minding my own business—"

"Don't give me that, Bert Klausen. You're almost as bad a liar as Russ. Now, you better tell me, 'cause I'll find out sooner or later."

"Oh, all right," he said, "I'll tell you what I know. But don't you let on to Russ that I blabbed. He'd be plenty put out with me."

"I won't say anything." She eagerly pulled a chair closer to the stove and sat.

"Her name's Sydney Baines and she's a private investigator. She came here asking Russ a whole lot of questions about his parentage. Wanted to know if he had a mother named Winifred. He said no, but didn't volunteer any further information. Fact is, he knew he was the one she was lookin' for, but he tried to convince her otherwise."

"Interesting," Winnie said, somewhat relieved to know that Russ's story wasn't entirely manufactured. Apparently she was stalking him, sort of. "What do you suppose it all means?"

"I don't know for sure," Bert said, "but if I had to guess, I'd say it had something to do with your life back in Vegas. Which probably means Russ did the right thing, scaring her off."

"Well, maybe so," Winnie said. If any of her old so-called friends were trying to track her down, looking for a handout, they were out of luck. She didn't have much money to give out anymore. She'd foolishly squandered much of the settlement Sammy had given her.

But her shop was bought and paid for, as was her little house. She did okay. Years ago she'd never have guessed she could be happy living such a normal, small-town life. But she'd found the contentment here in Linhart that had eluded her in Vegas and Dallas, despite the diamonds, parties and fancy clothes.

"I think Russ didn't scare her off, though," Winnie said. "They're both missing, so I think they must be together."

"It's none of our business," Bert said, which was so out-of-character for Bert to say. She knew he knew something more, something he didn't want her to know.

"Of course it's our business. This is Russ we're talking about. Will you let me know the moment you hear anything, about either of them?"

"'Course I will, Winnie."

"Thanks." Winnie looked around the store, trying to come up with a believable excuse for going into Russ's office to snoop. "Long as I'm here, I think I'll use Russ's computer and catch up on my e-mail."

"Don't you have a computer?" Bert asked suspiciously.

"The cold weather has frozen up the phone lines or something. My Internet has been out all day."

"Russ's computer is still turned on from yesterday. I don't touch them evil machines."

Winnie had to smile. Bert had embraced the cell phone, because it allowed him to gossip more efficiently, but he didn't trust computers.

She went to the office and Nero followed her, probably sensing she was up to no good. The dog's instincts were incredible. As she sat at Russ's desk, Nero sat beside her, watching her vigilantly. She reached down and scratched him on his neck.

"Now, Nero, I'm not doing anything that would hurt your master. You know I'd never do that. I'm just gonna Google this Sydney Baines and make sure she's not some criminal out to fleece us down to our underwear."

She got a lot of hits on Sydney Baines, the most intriguing of which was a Web site for Baines & Baines, a company that described itself as being in the "heir-finding" business. Hmm. She'd never heard of such a thing, but it sounded like maybe Sydney reunited family members. Could she be one of those people who tracked down children who'd been put up for adoption and matched them up with their natural mothers? She'd seen a show about that on the Discovery Channel.

She was about to investigate further when Bert appeared at the office door. "Betty just called and said you have a customer."

"Oh, shoot." She quickly closed down the browser so Bert couldn't see what she was doing. Winnie refused to turn down business, not on a day like today. She'd have to continue looking into this matter another time.

But maybe Betty would know something about heir-finding. Or she could ask her son, who was an attorney in Houston.

THE DAY PASSED TOLERABLY WELL, Sydney thought as she mixed up some instant grits for dinner, following Russ's instructions. She'd never imagined she would like something called *grits,* but with enough gravy and salt they weren't bad. Russ was an imaginative cook and he managed to turn out some pretty decent meals from the meager supply of cans and boxes in the kitchen cabinets. Certainly better than she could do.

Besides the time-consuming task of tending the fire and meal preparation, she and Russ had played Monopoly, put together a jigsaw puzzle and talked about everything and nothing. He was far more intelligent and well-read than she'd first thought, judging from just his job and his clothes. Although he hadn't graduated from college, he obviously read voraciously and was curious about everything. He'd read more of the classics than she had, that was for sure.

He loved history and wars and generals and naval battles, which she supposed was a guy thing, because her dad liked the same sort of stuff. He could name dates and places better than any history teacher she'd ever had.

Russ was passionate about his outdoor pastimes and he'd entertained her with stories of bears and coyotes, white-water mishaps, camping nightmares, encounters with all kinds of weather including tornadoes, which sounded terrifying. She'd found herself actually wishing she was a little more outdoorsy-adventuresome. She normally thought of herself as brave and daring, but with the exception of the chow, she'd never faced down any critter more threatening than a philandering husband.

Russ asked her about her work as a private investigator and she regaled him with some of her more memorable cases, like the time a cheating husband had caught her with a camera in the bushes behind his house and she'd wound up in jail, or the time she'd been investigating a routine workman's-comp-fraud case and found herself uncovering a major drug-smuggling operation.

So, yes, the day had gone far better than she'd expected. But there'd been no repeat of the kiss and no mention made of it.

Sydney was beginning to think she'd imagined the attraction between them, except that every once in a while she caught Russ looking at her with so much heat in his gaze that they didn't need a woodstove.

In truth, she'd spent quite a bit of her own time watching him covertly, imagining him naked. Imagining what it would feel like to touch him bare skin to bare skin rather than bundled in all these winter clothes.

She knew it was ridiculous. She and Russ were polar opposites and the only reason their worlds had intersected at all was because he happened to be the unwilling center of a case she'd been desperate to solve. Now that he'd refused to take the money, their business was concluded. She would go back to her life in New York and their paths would never cross again.

Any liaisons they made would, by necessity, be temporary and she'd already decided she didn't want a one-night stand. Still, that didn't mean she couldn't think about it. Which she did—a lot.

"I have a favor to ask," Russ began suddenly just as they sat down to dinner. "I know you don't owe me, but I have to ask anyway." He was unusually intense, and she got the feeling he'd been thinking about this favor for a while, and that it was important to him.

"Ask away. I'm not vindictive and if I can help, I will. What is it?"

"I'd like you to keep my identity confidential. If word got around that Sammy Oberlin's heir had refused ten million dollars, it would create all kinds of problems."

Sydney gave herself a moment to think about it. If she talked about this case to anyone, the news would spread like wildfire among private investigators. Every heir-finder in the country would camp out on Russ's doorstep, waving a contract in his face and begging him to sign. Reporters, too. The story was too irresistible to ignore.

The fact was, she hadn't planned on telling anyone. Why advertise her failure to bring the case to a satisfactory conclusion? But mostly, she didn't want her father to know. Lowell might be proud of Sydney for solving the case, but he would be crushed that she came so close to saving Baines & Baines, yet ultimately failed.

"I won't say a word," she said, "on one condition."

Wariness flashed across his face. "What?"

"Could you just tell me why you don't want the money? The real reason? I promise I won't try to change your mind. But I know you haven't told me the whole story."

# Chapter Eleven

Russ put down his fork and sighed. "It's because of my mother."

Sydney waited for him to continue.

"Winnie was a showgirl. She was beautiful—still is, but back then she was spectacular. She landed a job at the Clover—Sammy's casino, the Four-Leaf Clover—when she was twenty, but she had only one goal in mind. She intended to catch the eye of a millionaire and marry him. When Sammy Oberlin himself started paying attention to her, she thought she'd died and gone to heaven. She didn't care that he was twenty years older than her or that he treated her like a possession. She wanted the ring on her finger and an end to all her money problems."

Sydney knew the type. She'd gone to college with more than one girl whose only aim was to nab a Harvard Law School student so she could live in a big house, drive a Mercedes and never have to work again.

She wondered if Russ thought *she* was that type. And come to think of it, she'd been acting like money was the solution to all problems, when she well knew it wasn't.

"Sammy put her up in a nice apartment, but he wouldn't

move her into his house. And he wouldn't marry her, not even when she deliberately got herself pregnant with me. But he paid her well. She had the clothes, the car, the jewelry. She also had a cocaine habit, a gambling addiction and a lot of shallow friends who used her because she could buy them booze and drugs and they could hang out at her place.

"Then one day, it wasn't enough. Winnie threatened to break things off with Sammy unless he married her. So he did—in a bogus ceremony that was never registered with the state."

"That's how I found you," Sydney said. "The bogus wedding records. You were, what, about three at the time?"

He nodded. "I don't remember it. So they were supposedly married, but Sammy still wouldn't move Mom in with him."

"And she put up with that?"

"For a while. Eventually she got tired of his lies and she wanted to leave. But by then she was so addicted to the high-flying lifestyle, she couldn't. The idea of having to get a job, a real job—her showgirl days were over—terrified her.

"Then one day, Sammy made the decision for her. He'd fallen in love with one of Mom's so-called friends and wanted to marry her, which of course infuriated Mom even more since by then she'd figured out her marriage wasn't legal."

"Paula," Sydney added.

"Right. But Sammy had to get me and Mom out of the picture. I think I already told you that part. He paid us off to move far, far away."

"How old were you then?" This story both fascinated and repulsed Sydney. She'd gotten the idea that Sammy Oberlin wasn't a kind and gentle soul, but it sounded as if he was downright cruel to string along a woman—the mother of his child—for years on end.

"I was twelve. We moved to Dallas, which was far enough away to suit Sammy. Mom thought living in the town where Neiman Marcus was born would be the ultimate. But it turned into a nightmare. Sammy paid Mom a chunk of money to go away and she seemed intent on spending it as fast as she could. But life in the fast lane caught up with her. After her third trip to rehab, social services took me away from her."

"Oh, Russ." Sydney couldn't imagine how hard it must have been for a twelve-year-old boy to watch his mother self destruct.

"It was the best thing that could have happened, a wake-up call of sorts. Mom decided to move back to her hometown and live with her mother. She sobered up, regained custody and she took what remained of Sammy's settlement to buy the Cut 'n' Curl and go to beauty school. It was the first time I can remember that she set a goal and actually stuck with it. She was working harder than she ever had and for the first time in her life she was happy."

"So because of that…you think having money is bad?" Sydney wasn't going to try to change his mind. She'd promised. But she did want to understand.

"Money *is* bad for Winnie. Even though *she* knows it's bad for her, she still plots out big-bucks schemes. She's only had one real relapse, when my grandmother died and left her some cash. Not a whole lot, but enough. She took off for the casinos in Shreveport. I got a call a week later from the police. She'd lost it all—more than twenty thousand dollars—gambling. Got into a drunken brawl at a casino. Thankfully they agreed to drop the charges if I would take Winnie home."

"How old were you *then?*"

Russ had to think. "Nineteen? Something like that."

"Okay, let me see if I understand. Your mom's quality of

life is much higher when she doesn't have access to wads of cash. But the inheritance would be strictly yours. Winnie isn't mentioned in the will."

"So you think I could inherit ten million dollars and not share? I shudder to think what my life would be like. Winnie would see an endless supply of cash—and her son, standing in the way. Try to imagine it. She would be pestering me constantly, just like she did Sammy. She'd want a new car, a mink coat, a vacation. And if I didn't give it to her, I'd be a selfish pig. Even if I gave it all away to charity, she would be furious that I couldn't spare her a measly million or two. But I believe a million dollars would kill her. Hell, twenty thousand nearly did."

Russ shook his head. "We've built a great life in Linhart, but it wouldn't take much to ruin that forever. I won't do that, not to myself, not to Winnie."

Finally, Sydney understood. Russ was protecting his mother, the only real family he had. Just as Sydney was trying to save her father. The same money that could put her father's life back together could very well destroy Winnie's—and Russ's.

She reached across the table and squeezed his hand. "Okay."

With that one word, she conveyed her total understanding and acceptance of his situation. And everything changed between them—everything. Gone were the suspicions, the antagonism, the frustrations that had marred their earlier encounters, leaving nothing but the desire that had been simmering beneath the surface from the moment they'd laid eyes on each other.

"You're, uh, soup's getting cold," he said, his voice a little rough.

She hadn't taken a single bite, she'd been so focused on

Russ's story. "I'm not really that hungry." Not for food, anyway. She was hungry for connection. Now that they'd forged this thread of understanding, she longed for more. Clearing the air between them had cleared the way for true intimacy.

Provided Russ felt the same way.

He released her hand and stood suddenly, his chair scraping harshly against the floor. His gaze never left hers as he walked around the table. She quaked at the intensity of his gaze, the purpose in his movements as he pulled her chair out, with her still in it, and helped her stand.

"Thank you for understanding," he said.

"Thank you for telling me. I know it can't be easy, delving into such painful memories."

"No, I'll tell you what's not easy. Standing here and refraining from ripping your clothes off."

Okay, he got points for honesty. She straightened the collar of his shirt. "So why are you refraining? Yesterday you took off my shoe. In some countries, that means we're married."

He grinned, but only for a moment, because he soon had her in his arms and was kissing her with an intensity that literally stole her breath. She was light-headed and she clung to him to keep from falling. He smelled faintly of smoke from the fire and it was sexier than any high-priced designer cologne.

He broke the kiss and froze, looking off into space. "There's a problem."

"What?" No, no problems. Please. Tomorrow would be soon enough to deal with those.

"Birth control."

"Don't you have something here?" she asked, slightly desperate.

"Never brought a woman here. But maybe…" He pulled his wallet from his back pocket and opened it. "Yes."

Oh, thank goodness.

Without further ado he swept her up into his arms and carried her to the bedroom.

Russ couldn't believe this was happening. How had a woman he'd tricked and lied to transformed into a willing lover? He didn't deserve any consideration from her, but he wasn't stopping to question it, not aloud. He just wanted her naked.

The cabin had warmed up during the day, thanks to a lot of winter sun. So though the bedroom was the coldest room in the cabin, it wasn't nearly as inhospitable as it had been yesterday—and he wanted to make love to Sydney in a real bed.

The bed was unmade; neither of them had touched it since Russ had carried Sydney to the sofa the previous night. He set Sydney on it then found the light in the dark room and turned it on. He wanted to see her when he made love to her.

When he turned back to her, she was working on the buttons of her faded flannel shirt—an old shirt of his, actually, but it looked a helluva lot better on her.

"I thought you wanted me to undress you," he teased, taking over the job of removing her shirt. Underneath she wore a silky bra the color of the inside of a shell, with lacy half cups that allowed her shadowy nipples to peek through.

She looked so pretty in the sexy garment, he almost didn't want to take it off. But before he could even figure out how it fastened, she unclasped the front hook and shrugged out of it.

"Too slow." Then she surprised him by reaching for his jeans and unfastening the buttons with unwavering purpose. No hesitation there.

Lord, he loved a woman who knew her mind, who craved sex and enjoyed it as much as he did.

Given the layers of clothes they'd been wearing for warmth, they undressed in record time. Russ fluffed the covers up and urged Sydney to climb under where they could be warm and cozy, and he followed her.

For a few moments he just held her, letting her get accustomed to his body next to hers, enjoying every inch of her soft skin pressed against his. He soon couldn't resist kissing her again. She was responsive to his every touch and he explored her curves with his hands and mouth, pressing his face against her belly, blowing on her nipples, feeling her every shiver and sigh down to his marrow.

Sydney had never been made love to like this before. Though obviously fully aroused, Russ seemed in no hurry to get anyplace special. He explored her the way she might take in the sights, sounds and smells of an outdoor market, darting from booth to booth, tasting a sample of an orange here, a cantaloupe there, delighting in a pyramid of shiny red apples, feeling the texture of an avocado skin.

She got into the spirit of his style of lovemaking. She nibbled his earlobe and buried her fingers in his hair, pressed her nose against his neck and smelled the down-to-earth scents of soap, shaving cream and smoke.

Just when she thought she might explode with the fury of her desire for him, for every part of him, he dipped his finger inside her.

"Oh," she said, as if she'd just made a discovery, for in a way she had. Nothing had ever felt quite like this before. "What are you doing?"

"Having fun."

"I know, but…ohhh. Do you want me to…aren't we…" Her body tensed as her climax hit her full force, with swirling colors and a swooshing in her ears, and for a moment she thought she'd had a stroke or something because she went away for a bit, but if this was dying, she was all for it.

"That's it," Russ soothed, "let it go, don't hold back."

"Trust me," she gasped, "I'm not." He hadn't left her with enough control to do anything but accept what he was doing to her.

As the ripples of pleasure slowed and her body relaxed, she realized Russ was just holding her.

"That was hardly fair."

"No?" He raised up on one elbow and looked at her curiously.

"You took advantage."

"You're right, that's not fair. So I'll let you take advantage of me now."

"I can't move."

"I bet you can."

And sure enough, he was right. He started playing with her hair, then kissing her and in a few short minutes she was writhing beneath him as if she hadn't been so recently and so incredibly satisfied.

He pulled away only long enough to take care of protection. When he finally entered her she was crazy with passion for him, and she surprised herself by reaching another peak just as he did, as if somehow their minds had merged along with their bodies and all sensations were shared.

Finally they fell into an exhausted heap and slept like hibernating bears, but early in the morning, long before sunrise, they woke and did it all over again.

Sydney knew she would never think of sex the same way again.

"Is it always like this for you?" she asked later as they lay entwined under a down comforter, their breathing in sync.

"Good gravy, no. This was…life altering."

Of course he would say that and she knew her question had sounded like she was looking for reassurance. But she'd been genuinely curious. She'd read all the books. She thought she knew her way around the bedroom. But making love with Russ was something else. Something else, indeed.

SYDNEY DOZED AGAIN, and when she woke, the sun was up and she was alone in bed. "Russ?"

"Out here," he called from the main room. "You were sleeping soundly, so I went ahead and showered. I have a surprise for you."

"Unless it's bacon and eggs I'm not getting up," she called back, figuring he was concocting one of his imaginative meals.

"This has nothing to do with food."

Hmm, that had possibilities. She hopped out of bed, too late remembering her injured ankle. But it didn't hurt as much as before when she put weight on it. She was able to limp as opposed to hop. She grabbed her discarded shirt from last night and shoved her arms into the sleeves, then left the bedroom to see what Russ was up to.

She found him in the bathroom, pouring a pot of hot water into the tub. He'd made a hot bath for her. It was even full of bubbles.

It was such a sweet gesture, it made her eyes fill with tears.

She quickly dashed them away with the back of her hand, not wanting Russ to see. "Thank you," she managed.

The tub was short, but it was deep, and if she bent her knees she could immerse herself all the way to her neck in the steaming water. Russ made her bath even more pleasant by scrubbing her back and shampooing her hair for her. She loved having her hair washed and she fully indulged in the luxury of Russ's strong fingers massaging her scalp. He occasionally placed a kiss on her shoulder or ear, something the shampoo girl at her salon rarely did.

"Mmm, why don't you join me," she said lazily as he rinsed the last of the soap from her hair.

"I don't think we'd both fit in that tub," he reminded her. "Anyway, much as I'd love to dally, we need to get moving if we want to get home today. Some of the ice melted yesterday, but it's still going to be slow going. How's your foot?"

"Better," she said as he dried her off. "I think with the boot laced tight to provide some support and a walking stick for balance, I can make it. I'm not sure I can carry a pack, though."

"I can carry what we'll need."

Yesterday she'd been impatient to see the last of this place, but today she hated the thought of leaving. Yeah, it was rustic, but Russ had made staying here seem like a grand adventure.

She knew, too, that when they returned to civilization, their romantic interlude would come to an end. She had to suck it up and deal with reality. Loathe as she was to call this a one-night stand, that was exactly what it was. A spectacular one, but still…

Russ didn't disappoint her with breakfast. He fixed oatmeal with walnuts and raisins, not the instant kind out of an envelope, either. Sydney savored her last cozy meal with Russ. Then she stuffed her feet into her new hiking boots, wrapped herself in her borrowed jacket, gloves, knit hat and scarf, and prepared for the grueling hike.

RUSS HAD TO HAND IT TO SYDNEY, she didn't complain. Though she took every steep incline on her butt rather than risk depending on her iffy ankle to support her, she bore it all stoically, with only an occasional hiss or ladylike groan.

She even asked him a few questions about the wildlife after spotting raccoon prints in the mud and hearing a birdcall drifting on the wind.

"The only birds I ever see are pigeons, sparrows and starlings," she said glumly.

"Pigeons aren't so bad. Everybody hates them, but did you know they mate for life?"

"No, I didn't know that." She sounded surprised. "But when I was a little girl, I watched a pair build a nest and raise babies right outside my window. They nested under the eaves of our garage. I remember admiring how tirelessly they took care of the babies."

He was actually pleased to hear she took some interest in nature and wildlife. Maybe they weren't quite as opposite as he'd first thought. Yeah, they lived in different places, but they'd found common ground.

Oh, hell, who was he kidding? They'd found common ground in the bedroom and he was trying to rationalize the fact he'd slept with her when they both knew it was going nowhere. Though neither of them had whispered a word about anything long-term, he was still old-fashioned enough to feel he'd taken advantage of her. Especially since it was his fault she'd been stranded at the cabin in the first place.

It was really too damn bad. Because despite everything, they'd gotten along remarkably well. They'd found lots of things to talk about. But their geographic differences were too big to overcome. Maybe it was selfish of him, but he'd made a home in Linhart and he wasn't going to budge.

And he could hardly expect her to uproot her life. She had a business and a sick father back in New York.

Every time he looked at her, he felt an ache in his chest that troubled him. As short as the time was they'd had together, he suspected she was going to be harder to get over than any of the others. Much harder.

# Chapter Twelve

What should have been a three-hour hike took them six. It was actually closer to five miles than four, despite what he'd originally told Sydney. The last section of trail was the slowest, even though the terrain was flatter, because Sydney's ankle was starting to hurt more after having been put through so much abuse. But given that the trail was still slippery, she wouldn't let Russ carry her.

"You'll fall and then we'll both go down on our heads," she'd said. "I can make it, if you'll just let me go slowly."

He'd let her go, he thought, as slowly as she wanted. Because once they were back in Linhart, she would climb into her BMW and drive out of his life forever and he'd just as soon delay that event.

The final creek crossing was the most difficult; the water had risen in the past couple of days, and falling in meant a good soaking and instantaneous hypothermia. Russ insisted on taking Sydney's hand as they crossed the slippery log, though if she fell she would probably pull him right in with her.

Somehow, they made it across without mishap. And a

few minutes later, his Bronco came into view, parked exactly where he'd left it, partially covered with melting ice.

"Man, I hope your heater works," Sydney said, picking up her pace slightly now that the end was in sight. "The boots kept my feet warm, but everything else is numb."

"The heater in my car is like a blast furnace," he assured her. "But I wonder what I did with the keys."

"You're joking, right?" The look of panic she gave him was priceless.

"I'm joking." He reached into his jacket pocket and extracted the keys, walking to the passenger side to open the door for Sydney. But before he did, he turned to face her.

"I want to say something before we get back to town and everything gets crazy."

"O-okay," she said, looking apprehensive.

"It's just that…I know this was hardly your idea of a dream getaway weekend, but I had fun. I enjoy being with you. And not just when you're naked, either."

She actually blushed. It might have just been the effect of the cold wind on her face, but he found it charming anyway.

"I'm sorry I'm such an obstinate ass about the money—"

"No, let's not go there," she said quickly. "We've said all there is to say about the money. I do understand."

"Then you're an extraordinarily understanding woman." He wanted to take her in his arms and kiss her until they were both out of breath, kiss her until she agreed not to hurry back to New York. But he didn't like his chances. So he settled for a long hug and a less-than-passionate kiss on the forehead.

"I'm glad I met you, Sydney Baines."

"I'm not gone yet."

Yeah, but she would be. They always left eventually. He'd just always recovered and moved on. He wasn't sure he could this time.

As soon as Sydney was safely buckled into her seat, she wasted no time in locating her cell phone, which she'd tucked into her pocket, and turned it on. A couple of minutes later she had a decent signal and she punched in her father's office number. She was pleased when he answered. At least he was going in to work without her badgering him.

"Hey, Dad, it's me!"

"Sydney? Jeez Louise, girlie, I been worried sick about you. You okay?"

"Fine, I'm fine. I was stuck in a place that didn't have any phones and no cell service. Aunt Carol called and told you not to worry, didn't she?"

"You kidding? We were both worried sick. You better call her and let her know you're alive. She's minutes away from calling the National Guard."

Oh, great. "I'll call her in a minute. So what's up with you?"

"Same as usual. Bills and more bills."

"Don't do anything with them," Sydney cautioned her father. "Just stack them up and leave them on my desk. I have a system. I'll deal with everything soon as I'm back."

"Yeah, but they're threatening to cut off the Internet."

"They won't cut it off." Not till the end of the month, anyway, and she'd send them a check by then.

Lowell chuckled, an unusual sound for him. "You sound just like your mother sometimes. She used to juggle the bills like a cardsharp."

Sydney considered that a high compliment. Usually all she heard from Lowell was how she couldn't do anything as well as her mother. He often thanked her for stepping in to help at Baines & Baines and never intentionally insulted her. It was just that he missed his wife so much and each thing Sydney did that was slightly different from the way Shirley did it was a reminder of her absence.

"So, other than the bills, how are you?" Sydney asked.

He sighed. "Oh, you know, just passing time."

"Working on any new cases?"

"Found a guy who'd lost track of a security deposit. Made a whopping fifty bucks."

"Well, that's something."

Really, it was encouraging. Usually his depression didn't allow him to focus the way he used to. He rarely brought any case to its conclusion. But it had been almost a year since her mother's death, and Sydney was ever hopeful that with a few nudges from her, Lowell would catch the heir-finding fever again.

"I'll try to get home tonight," Sydney said. "If I can't, I'll call."

They said their goodbyes and Sydney disconnected, her heart aching. When she returned to New York, her father would have to file for bankruptcy and she dreaded breaking the news to him.

"Everything okay?" Russ asked.

"Hmm? Oh, it's just my dad. He sounds really sad and lonely and not much interested in work. I remember when he and my mom used to race each other to the phone. They always competed to see who could bring in the most business each month. They put up a bar chart on the wall and crowed each time they got to fill in another square. Now he doesn't even bother to answer the phone. He just lets it roll to voice mail or lets me handle everything. He won't tackle any of the challenging cases anymore."

Her voice caught in her throat and she quickly swallowed back tears. No more, not now. It was thinking about the bar chart that did it. She'd finally taken it down last month and Lowell hadn't spoken to her for a solid week.

"I'm sorry," Russ said softly. "I wish I knew what to say."

He could say he would accept his inheritance. Money didn't solve everything, but it would be a helluva lot easier to deal with her father's grief if they didn't have to dodge bill collectors.

Sydney quickly called Aunt Carol and get her voice mail. Probably having her hair done, Sydney thought.

Next she called her travel agent. Most everyone made their reservations online these days, but Baines & Baines had been using Debra Grogan's agency for twenty or more years. Debra was a miracle worker and even in the most trying circumstances could usually figure out a way to get her clients from point A to point B.

"Kiddo, I'm afraid you're out of luck," Debra said after searching fruitlessly for a flight from Austin to New York that departed that evening. "Because of the weather delays down there, everything's booked solid. Earliest I can get you on a plane is ten-thirty-two tomorrow morning, and even then, you'll be routed through Timbuktu."

"Okay, go ahead and book it," Sydney said, not all that disappointed. She didn't want to have to rush, anyway, and Lowell had sounded reasonably calm.

"I figured you might have trouble getting a flight," Russ said. "First hint of ice or snow in Texas and everything shuts down."

"It's okay. I can visit with my aunt—I hardly ever see her."
Then Sydney happened to look down at herself. "But I can't
go to her place looking like this. She's one of those proper
Southern ladies who wouldn't dream of stepping outside to
collect the mail without a perfect manicure and her face fully
made up." Sydney examined her ragged nails and chipped nail
polish and moaned. "What have I done to myself?"

"I happen to think you look pretty good." Which was a little surprising. It was the fancy clothes, the elegant hair and
the long, polished nails that had first drawn him to Sydney.
He'd never imagined he would find a woman wearing his cast-
off clothes and a hairdo like a bird's nest to be exciting. But,
honestly, she was the most exciting woman he'd ever known
no matter what she was wearing.

"Thanks, but you've had sex with me. That completely in-
validates any and all opinions."

Russ laughed. "I've got an idea. Since you don't have to
leave till tomorrow, why don't you stay on another day? I'll
take you out for a first-class steak dinner, dancing, the works.
I'll even buy you a new dress. You can stay with me."

"You wouldn't mind?" she asked, thrilled, as well as blatantly curious about where he lived.

"Mind?" He laughed.

Sydney smiled. "All right, then, I'll stay. Dancing is probably out, but I suppose a steak dinner is the least you can do
after I was forced to endure a breakfast of succotash and
pork-and-beans."

"The food wasn't all bad."

"Not once you were there to cook. But it wasn't steak."

They'd reached Main Street. Russ pulled up behind
Sydney's car. "Go check out of the B and B and meet me back

at the store. You can follow me home and we'll get all gussied up at my place and we can paint the town red. Well, as red as Linhart gets."

"Sounds like a plan."

After retrieving her purse from Russ's backpack, Sydney waved goodbye, then drove back to Gibson Street to the Periwinkle. The Milhaus sisters were kind enough not to charge her for the extra nights, since the only thing enjoying the B and B's hospitality was her suitcase.

"It's not your fault you were stranded by the storm," Miss Gail said, holding one of the fat cats and stroking it. "We enjoyed having you and we hope you'll come back."

"Maybe I will." The possibility cheered her.

She pulled up in front of the Linhart General Store once again, but she didn't go inside because she spotted something that interested her. Out of the corner of her eye she saw that the Cut 'n' Curl was just across the street and down the block, and Sydney needed a manicure in the worst way. Hopefully, someone at the salon knew how to do nails and would take her as a walk-in. If she didn't get a manicure in the next twenty minutes she was going to go crazy.

Walking into the Cut 'n' Curl was like taking a trip back to 1962. The salon was all done in pink and aqua, with three stylist stations in the front room and a row of old-fashioned hair dryers in the back. The smell of permanent solution hung heavy in the air, as did copious amounts of Aquanet hairspray.

Sydney had scarcely walked through the door when she was accosted by a woman with the biggest bleached-blond hair she'd ever seen. "Well hellooooooo there," the woman said. Despite her retro hairstyle, she was entrancingly beautiful. She had big, dark brown eyes, flawless skin and a long Audrey Hepburn neck.

She also had breasts the size of cantaloupes, the cleavage of which she displayed proudly in a low-cut, tight pink uniform. And she was tall—probably close to six feet; most of it legs.

Could this woman possibly be Russ's mother? She didn't look old enough.

"What can we do for you today?" the woman asked with a big smile.

Sydney stared at the two women who were having their hair done by the other stylists, who also wore pink uniforms. She hadn't teased and sprayed her hair like that since her role as Marie Antoinette in her high-school play.

"I'm in desperate need of a manicure," Sydney said, showing the woman her pitiful nails. "Can you take a walk-in?"

"Honey, for those nails, I'll make room in my schedule. What have you been doing, climbing trees?"

Sydney relaxed, smiling at the woman's frank appraisal. "Something like that."

"You just come on back to the manicure table and we'll get you soaking. What about a pedicure, too? We got a special going, half-price on the toes if you do the fingers. I know it's winter and no one sees your feet, but it'll make you feel pretty on the inside just knowing your toenails are all bright and shiny"

"Okay, sure." The price list was posted by the front door, and this place was a bargain compared to what she was used to in New York. She could indulge.

"I'm Winnie, by the way," the woman said as she led Sydney to the manicure table, confirming her suspicions. "Would you like a trim, too? Maybe a shampoo and blowout? Don't be put off by all the big hair. Lots of the ladies around here won't give up their permanent waves or the Dolly Parton look." She patted her own shaggy bouffant. "But we can do the latest hairstyles, too."

Much as Sydney would love to indulge in a whole day of pampering after her backwoods adventure, she didn't have that much time. "Not today," she said to the affable Winnie.

"Not even a facial? I've got this new cucumber mask that I guarantee will leave your face feeling like a baby's bottom."

"Is that what *you* use?" Sydney asked as she unlaced her hiking boots. They didn't look new anymore. She'd broken them in but good. "I couldn't help noticing how pretty your skin looks."

"Well, thank you, hon!" Winnie smiled ear-to-ear, revealing perfectly straight, blindingly white teeth. "I've always used a lot of sunscreen, that's the key." She disappeared into a back room, and a short time later reappeared with a footbath full of warm water. She plugged it in as Sydney rolled up her jeans and eased her poor, abused feet into paradise.

"My word," Winnie said, "what did you do to your foot?"

"I sprained my ankle," she said. "A hiking mishap."

"Don't tell me my idiot son took you out into the woods and tried to get you to hug trees."

Uh-oh. Apparently Winnie had her ear to the ground, because she knew Sydney and Russ had been together. Sydney had better tread carefully. "Well, sort of."

"I swear, that boy doesn't have a clue how to impress a woman. Couldn't he see the moment you stepped out of that car wearing those pretty clothes that you weren't an out-doorsy type?"

"Oh, but I'm not…that is, we weren't…" Oh, hell. How was she going to explain this? She couldn't breathe a word about her true purpose or she would break her promise to Russ, not to mention possibly ruin someone's life.

Then a thought occurred to her. If Winnie thought Sydney and her son were involved romantically, there would be no need to explain her presence in Linhart. And it wouldn't be a lie at this point. She and Russ were, after all, going out on a real date tonight, even if it would be their last hurrah.

"You don't have to pretend with me," Winnie said in a confidential whisper. "I'm not one of those mothers who thinks no woman is good enough for her son. Truth is, I'd like for Russ to settle down and give me a couple of grand-babies."

"It's not that serious!" Sydney blurted out. "I mean, we just met…we've only started…" Her face went hot. This was getting worse and worse. No matter what she said, it seemed to give the wrong impression. Winnie had to know she and Russ had spent a couple of nights together.

Winnie laughed. "Settle down, hon. I won't push, I promise. So other than ruining your ankle, did you enjoy the camping? Frankly I have no use for freezing in a tent and tinkling in the woods, but some people really seem to like it."

"It wasn't terrible," Sydney answered, realizing it was true. "You're right, I'm not really the outdoorsy type. But Russ made it fun. Besides, there was a cabin, not a tent. And a bathroom, once I found it. He's a good guy, your son."

"Oh, don't I know it," Winnie said. "We went through some hard times, him and me, back when I was young and stupid. He took care of me more than I did him. From the time he was a little bitty thing he was watching out for me—almost like he knew he was destined to be the strong one of the two of us."

"He obviously loves you a lot," Sydney said.

Winnie sniffed and Sydney wondered if she was crying. Maybe she was one of those women who cried at anything. But then she seemed to shake herself out of it. "What color did you want today, sweetie?"

Sydney chose a deep, dark red nail polish, which suited her mood. Then she lay back and let Winnie give her the facial and rub her feet. It had been so long since she'd pampered herself, or spent an afternoon gossiping with a female friend. She missed her mother and the long conversations they used to have, particularly during that last year, when she was ill.

By the end of the afternoon Sydney had the most beautiful hands and feet in the world—and a new friend. Winnie was nothing short of delightful, funny and painfully honest about herself. But Sydney sensed a vulnerability about her, a certain naïveté. She could just imagine how a fast-paced, me-first city like Las Vegas could chew Winnie up and spit her out.

By the time Sydney was done at the beauty shop, it was getting late. She hadn't brought any clothes with her that were suitable for a fancy restaurant, so she darted next door to Rose's Dress Shop. The clothes in the window looked very stylish and high quality to Sydney, so it was worth a shot.

With the help of the elderly proprietor, who had a keen eye and knew what would look good on Sydney's petite, slender frame, she picked out a slinky cocktail dress the color of a caramel apple. She had a pair of low-heeled pumps that would match perfectly and wouldn't put too much stress on her ankle. Despite the disaster of Baines & Baines's financial situation, her personal finances were still in decent shape—although nowhere near enough to pay off her father's debts—and she could certainly afford a dress.

It was dark and most of the businesses on Main Street were closing up by the time Sydney hurried across the street to meet Russ at the general store. She couldn't wait to see him again. And she was practically coming out of her skin as she considered spending another night with him. How in the world was she going to simply get in her car and drive to the airport tomorrow morning, never to see him again?

WINNIE WAS CLOSING THE BLINDS at the Cut 'n' Curl when she saw Sydney crossing the street with a large shopping bag from Rose's Dress Shop. Betty came over and joined her.

"What's she up to?"

"Just went shopping, apparently. She's putting her clothes and things into the trunk of her car. I wonder if she's leaving."

"She seemed nice. I was busy with Irma's highlights so I couldn't really eavesdrop, but it seemed like you two were having fun."

"She *is* nice," Winnie confirmed, which had surprised her. Usually it took some time to win over one of Russ's girl-friends. At first they were always reserved, ready to compete for Russ's affections. As if he didn't have enough to go around. She knew that secretly they thought her big hair was tacky and that she ought to dress more conservatively.

But she was who she was and she'd sensed total acceptance from Sydney. Or maybe that was just wishful thinking. If Russ did ever settle down, Winnie hoped she and her daughter-in-law could be friends.

"Nope, she's not leaving," Betty said. "She's going back

into the general store. Did she tell you anything more about why she's here?"

"She and Russ are involved, apparently, despite what Russ said. He took her on some wilderness adventure and she didn't run away screaming, so that's a good sign."

"I thought Bert told you she was here on business."

"He did. But he was being cagey about it. Come to think of it, Sydney was a little bit vague, too, about how she and Russ met. I mean, she's from New York."

"Yeah, well, I didn't have time to tell you before, but I talked to my son about this heir-finder business. Heir finders don't merely reunite loved ones. They find people who are due an inheritance but don't realize it and help them recover the funds—for a cut, of course."

"Oh. Ohhhh. That makes more sense. I should have asked her more about her work." Winnie's heart hammered inside her chest. Had someone left Russ some money?

She knew of only one person connected to Russ who'd died with any money to speak of. When news of Sammy's death had reached her a few years ago, Winnie hadn't spent much time mourning the bastard. She had sent some flowers and a generic note of sympathy for Paula, because they'd once been friends even if the witch had stolen her husband, but then she'd promptly forgotten about it.

Could Sammy have left Russ some money? It seemed unlikely. He'd never once treated Russ as anything but an inconvenience and an embarrassment. And wouldn't Paula have gotten in touch to let her know? Granted, they hadn't parted on the best of terms, but still.

"Betty, you're better at computers than I am. Would you help me look up some stuff?"

Fifteen minutes later, crowded into her tiny office, Winnie and Betty stared at the computer screen in shock.

"Ten million dollars. Sammy left Russ ten million dollars. My God. I'm going to be rich!"

"Uh, Winnie, honey, before you get carried away, the money is Russ's, not yours."

"He's my son, my only child," Winnie argued. "Of course he'll share with me." She closed her eyes, thinking of what all she could do with that kind of money. She'd buy the mink coat she'd always wanted, to replace the one she'd sold. And a brand-new Cadillac, the expensive kind, too, not a cheap one. Maybe a vacation to Paris. "I could have my own apartment in Paris!"

"Winnie, you're getting ahead of yourself."

"I have to call Eleanor. She's always rubbed it in that she doesn't have to work because her husband's so stinking rich. This'll shut her up. And Lisa Gerber, too. She practically laughed at me when I wanted to run for garden-club treasurer. Well, we'll see about that."

## Chapter Thirteen

Sydney drove her own car to Russ's house, following his Bronco. The road leading up to it was almost as bad as the one they'd taken into the woods before their hike, but that didn't surprise her. She couldn't see him living in some suburban subdivision. They were near a lake, she knew that, because she'd caught glimpses of the setting sun glistening on rippling water whenever there was a break in the trees.

But nothing prepared her for his house. It was fantastic—a redwood cabin on steroids. His property was right on the water, and she could just make out a private dock and a boathouse maybe a hundred steps from his front door. He opened the two-car garage and then pulled to the side, motioning with one hand that she should park the BMW there.

She slid the window open and he did the same. "I don't want to take your parking place," she said. Because the rest of the garage was filled with bicycles and kayaks and other sports paraphernalia, there was room for only one car.

"You're the one who has to get up early. It's supposed to rain in the morning and I want you to be warm and dry for your trip."

That was really sweet of him. Since she'd had enough of cold and wet for this century, she accepted his offer.

She opened her door to find Nero right there, waiting excitedly for her to exit the car. The dog did seem to like her, though she couldn't imagine why. She hadn't given him one bit of encouragement.

"Nero," Russ said sternly, "back off and let the lady move."

Sydney looked into the hound's sad, bloodshot eyes and she saw something there she'd never seen before. Nero suddenly had an identity, a personality. He was no longer merely a dog, to be lumped generically with all dogs. He was Nero, Russ's dog, the first dog to ever like her.

She reached out one tentative hand and patted the top of his head. His fur was warm and soft. He seemed to enjoy the attention.

"I guess he's not such a bad dog," Sydney said.

Russ looked as pleased as she'd ever seen him, which was saying a lot.

His house was no less impressive on the inside. The focal point was a great room with a fireplace in the center that heated both a den area and a dining room. A large kitchen opened out to both areas. A wall of glass looked out onto the deck and ultimately out to the lake. Everywhere were the earthy tones of wood and stone—the floors, the high-beamed cathedral ceiling, the walls. It was almost as if the house had spring directly from the earth without human intervention.

Russ took her on a brief tour while Nero followed them around, his toenails clicking against the wood floors.

"This is amazing."

"Thanks. I built a lot of it myself, though I had an architect friend refine my plans. Bert and a couple of the guys from town helped with some of the major stuff."

Sydney turned slowly, taking it all in. The furniture had a slightly worn, comfortable look, as did the rugs. The place didn't have the appearance of a professional decorator, but it all worked.

"Why don't you sit down and put your feet up?" Russ suggested. "I'll get us some wine and a snack. Our reservation isn't until eight-thirty, so we have time."

How civilized. A late dinner. So not everyone in Linhart opted for the early-bird special and went to bed with the chickens.

Russ showed Sydney to the most comfortable-looking chair in the den. She sat down with a sigh and put her feet on the footstool. Ah, heaven. She hadn't realized how much her ankle had been hurting until she got off it.

It took only a moment for Russ to get a fire going, with the help of a gas starter.

"Now, that's my kind of fireplace," Sydney said. "I think even I could start *this* fire. No kindling, no newspaper, no using a zillion matches."

"It's nice," Russ agreed. "It rarely gets cold enough down here that a fire makes sense. I'll be back in a minute."

She heard him going into the kitchen and rustling around. It sounded like maybe he was giving Nero food and water. Then she heard the unmistakable sound of a wine bottle being uncorked. He returned with two glasses filled with white wine and handed her one.

"Authentic Texas wine," he announced.

She eyed it dubiously. "No kidding?" It looked like normal wine. "What shall we toast to?"

Russ raised his glass. "To…civilization. Much as I love roughing it in the woods, I don't mind creature comforts, either."

"To civilization," Sydney agreed. They touched glasses and each took a sip of the wine. It was cold and dry and exactly what she needed. "Mmm, not half bad."

Russ sat on one end of the sofa. "I happened to look out the window at the store earlier and saw you coming out of Rose's dress shop. What did you think?"

Had he just "happened" to be looking? Or had he been watching for her? It pleased her enormously to think he'd been anxious for her to return.

"It's a very nice shop," she said. "Rose is a lovely lady and she helped me pick out the perfect dress for tonight, on sale."

"It must have taken you quite a while to find what you wanted," Russ said. "Either that, or it took you forever to get packed up and check out of the Periwinkle. I was starting to think you'd driven back to Austin after all."

"Oh, I didn't spend all that time shopping. I had my nails done." She wiggled her red nails at him.

Russ went very still. "You did?"

"Yes, and don't look like a scared rabbit. I met your mother and she's absolutely delightful. I did not breathe a word about money or Sammy Oberlin or anything like that. I'm afraid she got it into her head that I'm your new girlfriend and I didn't disabuse her of the notion. I thought it would be simpler for her to believe that. And it's a little bit true. I mean, we are going out on a date."

Russ relaxed. "So what did you talk about?"

"About the latest hairstyles and fashion and what it was like living in New York and the fact that she'd like grandbabies."

Russ pinched the bridge of his nose. "You're kidding."

"Has she not mentioned that to you?" Sydney asked innocently.

"Actually, no, she hasn't. I had no idea she'd ever be interested in being a grandmother. I thought the idea would horrify her if it ever happened."

"Oh, I expect it'll happen," Sydney said. "Some lucky girl will snag you and fill this house with little boys and girls. You can take them camping and teach them how to fish and canoe and survive on nothing but acorns and a book of matches."

Russ laughed.

Sydney wanted to cry.

The picture she'd painted was more than slightly appealing. She could easily see Russ with a little boy, one with his same gold-streaked hair, their heads bent over a fishing line as Russ taught his son how to bait a hook. What really hurt was imagining a little girl with her own features—something she knew could never be.

She felt an unexpected ache in her chest, which surprised her. She'd never felt a particular affinity for children and figured she simply wasn't born with a lot of maternal instincts. But for the first time in her life she knew she wanted to have children someday. She wanted to share that bond of parenthood with a good man, someone who would provide the nurturing and companionship that Russ himself had lacked as a child.

"Oh, I have some cheese and crackers to tide us over," Russ said suddenly. He set his wine down and jumped up, as if someone had lit his fuse. She wondered if the talk of children had made him feel any disquieting thoughts. He seemed the type of guy who would like kids, but maybe he wasn't.

She heard more rustling in the kitchen, but this time when he came back to the den he had a cutting board loaded up with some squares of cheddar cheese, a pile of wheat crackers and an apple sliced into thin wedges.

Sydney's stomach grumbled. The improvised lunch they'd shared on the trail—a couple of hastily chewed granola bars and some nuts and raisins—had been many hours ago, and she'd expended a lot of calories since then. She tried not to fall on the snack like a ravenous wolf.

"Be sure and save room for dinner," Rush cautioned her.

"Oh, don't worry, I'll find room for a good steak. Three days of camping food and I'm ready to go out and rustle up my own cow and eat it whole."

Sydney was feeling marginally human again. Her foot had stopped throbbing, too. But if they had dinner reservations at eight-thirty, she should get moving; she had some work ahead of her to get presentable.

Russ showed her to the master suite. The bath was five times the size of the tiny bathroom at the cabin. It was all done in navy blue tile with chrome accents, and the shower was definitely big enough for two. She thought briefly of inviting Russ to join her, but if she did they'd never make it to dinner. Maybe later.

Later? She was running out of later. She could spend many more days exploring Russ Klein, his body, his mind, his soul. A few hours weren't going to do it.

"You don't by any chance have a blow-dryer, do you?" she asked, looking at her bird's nest of a hairdo in the mirror. If she didn't make a concerted effort to straighten it, it went into a wild array of out-of-control curls.

"Actually, I do." He opened several drawers in the vanity until he came up with it.

"Hmm, what girlfriend left that behind?"

"How do you know it's not mine?"

She rolled her eyes. "Come on. You're just not the blow-dried type."

"Actually, her name was Deirdre. But she left it at my old place—she never stayed here. She was long gone by the time I moved in here."

Sydney felt a surge of jealousy that some other woman had enjoyed sleepovers with Russ. He'd been right, he was painfully honest. Most men wouldn't willingly reveal information about an old girlfriend.

But that unwelcome and inappropriate feeling quickly dissipated. That woman wasn't here now. She was. And she wasn't going to let her few remaining hours with Russ be wasted with petty jealousy.

Once she had the bathroom to herself, she washed the trail grime from her body, scrubbing until she was pink. She shampooed her hair again, even though it had been washed just that morning.

Thank God for Deirdre, Syndey thought with a smile as she dried her hair until it was smooth and almost straight.

She primped as much as she could with her travel make-up case from her purse. She slipped into the new dress and put on some understated gold jewelry. New stockings and her comfortable brown pumps completed her outfit. With one light spritz of perfume, she exited the bedroom suite and went looking for her man. Hers for the evening, anyway.

Sydney found Russ in the den, fiddling with the fire. And for a moment she just stopped and stared. He wore a charcoal gray wool suit that fit him perfectly, accentuating his height and his wide shoulders. The suit looked as nice as any she'd ever seen, as did the silk tie in muted blues and grays. His hair, still slightly damp from his shower, had been neatly combed. When she came closer, she saw that he'd shaved. A tiny nick along his jaw gave him away.

He straightened and held out his arms. "What do you think? Do I pass muster?"

"Oh, you pass, all right."

She wondered who picked out his clothes. The mysterious Deirdre?

She clenched her jaw. She was walking away and there would be other Deirdres. She didn't need to know, didn't want to think about them or about the man she'd always think of as the one who got away.

"You clean up good, too," Russ said, "but I already knew that." He held up his hand. "No, wait, let me state that more emphatically. You look fantastic and I will be sure to tell Rose she advised you well."

"Thank you." Sydney appreciated the compliment. She did feel pretty tonight and the fire in his eyes told her all she needed to know about how well her efforts had paid off.

"Ready to go?" he said.

"Absolutely. I'm not going to last long in these heels, so the sooner we can get to a table, the better."

The Lake Linhart Country Club wasn't actually in Linhart. It was across the lake from Russ's house. He showed Sydney the lights visible from his back door, but it was about a fifteen-minute drive to get there.

The club reeked of old money. Russ told her that a group of oil barons of another era had built this place as a private playground, but during the oil bust of the 1980s it had been sold and converted to a country club with membership open to anyone willing to pay the modest dues. It didn't feature the latest, most chic decor, but everywhere Sydney looked she saw quality, from the parquet floor to the wall sconces to the maître d's tuxedo.

"Mr. Klein, how nice to see you again so soon," the maître d' said. "Your table is ready."

"You must be a good customer."

"Actually, I do a lot of work for the club, organizing wilderness adventures for the members. I even teach kayaking and windsurfing. So they know me."

The dining room was small but elegantly appointed. They were led to a table right by a wall of windows, where they could look out onto the lake. The sky shimmered with stars. Sydney had never seen so many.

The evening was as perfect as any dinner date could be. The filet Sydney ordered was grilled to perfection; the red wine was hearty and seeped into Sydney's exhausted bones, relaxing her. Even the background music set just the right tone of intimacy.

They talked of anything and everything, carefully avoiding any mention of the future they wouldn't be sharing. They lingered over coffee late into the evening as their conversation dwindled to comfortable silence and they stared into each other's eyes.

Sydney tried to find hidden depths in Russ's eyes, answers to questions she hadn't yet asked. He reached across the table and took her hand, lightly kissing the knuckles. "Let's go home."

Oh, yeah. She couldn't stand up fast enough.

Once they were back inside the warm haven of Russ's home,

they took off their coats and then simply didn't stop undressing. Their discarded clothing left a trail from the front door to the bedroom as they kissed their way through the house.

A night-light softly illuminated their love nest, where the king-sized bed awaited. They hardly spoke a word; no words were necessary. They were so attuned to each other that Russ knew exactly where she wanted to be touched, how fast, how slow. In turn, her instincts guided her eager, hungry hands and mouth as she charted a body that was already becoming familiar to her. Thoughts of him would haunt her for a long time to come, she was sure.

When they came together it was like coming home, a place she'd been in her mind many times but hadn't even known she'd missed until now.

Their lovemaking seemed to go on in a timeless alternate universe and for a while Sydney forgot about deadlines and airports and bankruptcies and depressed fathers and sprained ankles. She forgot everything except loving this man in this time and this place.

Much later, as they lay entwined in the big bed, twisted sheets and blankets and pillows around them, Sydney realized with sudden clarity that she'd fallen in love. As preposterous as it seemed, she'd fallen in love with this exasperating, stubborn Texan with whom she outwardly had nothing in common.

She glanced at the illuminated dial on Russ's watch. She had to get up in three hours. Get up, throw on her clothes and drive away, probably never to see Russ again. How was she going to do it? Did she really have to?

If not for her father, she could choose to stay and explore this miraculous thing that had come into her life so unexpectedly. But Lowell—she couldn't leave Lowell to fend for himself. It was unthinkable.

At the thought of her father, she remembered she hadn't called to let him know she wasn't coming home tonight. Russ was asleep, snoring softly. She slipped out of his grasp, which was tenacious even in sleep. The room was cold and she had no nightgown or robe. So she improvised by locating Russ's discarded dress shirt and wrapping it around her. She hugged herself and inhaled deeply. The shirt smelled of him. Maybe she could steal it, take it home with her, put it in her bed so she could inhale of him at will.

She had it bad, all right.

She wondered where she'd left her purse. Nero was sprawled out in the entryway, snoring. After searching everywhere for her purse, she realized Nero was sleeping on it, using it for a pillow.

"Hey, you." She nudged him with her toe. The dog opened one tired eye, identified her as friend and wagged his tail. "Yeah, well, that cute act isn't going to get you very far if you've slobbered all over my suede purse."

She tugged her small clutch out from under the dog's head. Aside from a bit of dog hair, it didn't seem much worse for wear. She dug out her cell phone.

There were no messages, so her father hadn't called her. He must not be too worried. She decided, though it was the middle of the night, to call him. He would probably be asleep, although his sleep was iffy these days. But the message would be there for him when he woke up.

When her father picked up, she was so surprised that for a moment she didn't say anything.

"Sydney? Honey?"

"Oh, hi, Dad. I didn't expect you to answer. What are you doing up?"

"Just prowling the house. Couldn't sleep. Something wrong?"

"No, I just forgot to call and let you know I wasn't coming in until tomorrow. I was afraid you'd be worried." She wandered into the living room and curled up on the sofa.

"I figured getting a flight out would be near impossible with the weather, so I wasn't too worried. Are you at your aunt Carol's?"

"No, I'm… Oh, Dad, the most wonderful, terrible thing has happened. I'm in love."

"No kidding? So that's what this mysterious trip was all about."

"It didn't start out that way, but that's how it's finishing up."

"You don't sound completely happy. Don't tell me the fella doesn't love you back."

"I honestly don't know. It's just that, regardless of how he feels, he's here and I'm there and that makes things difficult."

"Well, now, it shouldn't," Lowell said. "Don't forget your mom and I were from different parts of the country, too. But we worked it out."

"Yeah, you moved to New York. But that's never going to happen in this case. Russ would never leave his precious Hill Country. And I wouldn't want him to. He wouldn't be happy in the city."

"Even with you?"

"Not even with me."

"Well, there must be some way to work it out. Couldn't you move down there?"

Sydney was surprised her father would suggest such a

thing. For the past year he'd been completely dependent on her and they both knew it. "Oh, I don't think so, Dad. New York is my home."

"Now, if you're just sticking around because you're worried about your old man, don't. I'll get by."

But he wouldn't. He needed her, at least for a while longer.

"We'll talk about it when I get back," she said. "I don't have to make any decisions right now."

"Sydney, honey, if you love this man, don't let him get away. Maybe it's an old-fashioned notion to believe in fate, but I do. I know there was one woman fated for me and I found her. Once I found her, I didn't let her go. Not till I had to, anyway." He paused and she knew he was struggling once again with his grief.

*Please don't let him start crying.* She couldn't stand it when her formerly invincible father resorted to tears.

To her surprise, however, he continued speaking, his voice clear and strong. "Don't let your life be filled with thoughts of what might have been. Don't settle for almost good enough."

Sydney swallowed hard at the reminder of the love between her parents. They'd been so different from each other and yet they'd had the happiest of marriages. Was it at all possible that she and Russ... Her heart beat a little faster just thinking of the possibilities.

Maybe she didn't have to say goodbye forever. Oh, but she didn't even know if Russ felt the same way. He might freak out if she told him how she felt. Lots of guys wanted nothing to do with love and commitment. Maybe there was a reason he'd reached his thirties without marrying—such as an aversion to commitment.

"Sydney, you still there?"

"Yeah, Dad. Just thinking about things. Are you taking the sleeping pills Dr. Stevens prescribed?"

"Nah. I'm not taking any of those pills anymore. I want to feel like myself again."

Sydney wasn't sure that was such a hot idea, but she had to admit, her dad sounded a little stronger than he had for a while. Maybe he was coming around.

Or maybe she was simply trying to justify her completely irrational desire to chuck everything and move to Texas to be with a man who might not even want her.

After concluding her call with her father, Sydney realized with a start that Nero was lying on the sofa next to her and she was patting him absently. "I bet you're not supposed to be on the furniture," she said. He yawned and rolled over, apparently wanting her to scratch his belly. "I like you, but I don't like you that much. Try not to take advantage."

## Chapter Fourteen

Russ awoke feeling pleasantly warm and drowsy, but something was missing. He reached beside him to find nothing but empty bed.

Damn it! If she'd slipped out of bed and sneaked away in the night, he was going to kill her. Maybe she wanted to skip the painful goodbye, but he'd been counting on a last coffee together. He'd wanted to give her a memorable send-off. No sense making it easy for her to walk out of his life.

He threw back the covers and leaped from the bed. The bathroom was dark.

As he exited the dimly lit bedroom he almost tripped over her shoes, then saw that her stockings and bra were still on the floor, right where they'd left them last night in their hurry to reach the bed.

Russ relaxed slightly. She wouldn't leave so fast she'd forget her clothes. But where was she? His experience with her morning habits was scanty, but he didn't peg her for a cheerful early riser.

He found her curled up on the sofa staring into the fire's dying embers, a cell phone in her hand—stroking Nero, who was stretched out beside her.

"Sydney?"

She and Nero jumped at the same time. Nero slinked off the couch and tried to become invisible.

"Yeah, you better hide."

"Sorry," Sydney said. "I figured he wasn't allowed on the furniture, but he ignored me when I told him to get down." She was wearing his shirt and nothing else. He liked the look. But he didn't like the sheen of tears in her eyes.

"Is something wrong?"

"I just couldn't sleep. I decided to call my father and let him know when to expect me home, since I forgot to do it earlier."

Even on New York time, it would still be an ungodly hour. "You called your father in the middle of the night?"

"I intended to simply leave a message. He turns off the ringer at night. But he was awake, so we talked for a bit."

"You're upset."

She waved away his concern. "No, I'm okay. We were just talking about Mom, that's all."

Russ sat down beside her and, conscious of the fact he wasn't wearing a stitch of clothing, grabbed a fleece throw he kept on the sofa and threw it over both of them. "I guess you still miss her a lot."

"Yeah. But it's Dad I'm worried about. He hasn't been the same since she died. I've helped as much as I could without losing all my own clients, but without my mom it's not enough. He's going to lose the business."

"What? You mean, bankruptcy?"

Sydney nodded. "I've put it off as long as I could. But Mom was sick for a while before she died and they lost some business then. When she got sicker, her medical bills really went through the roof, then their insurance, well, you know how it is for self-employed people. Since then it's only been getting worse. The budget only has so much give and it's given all it's going to."

"I'm sorry, Sydney. I can't imagine what it would be like to lose a business you've built up your whole life. I've put less than ten years into mine, but it's my lifeblood."

"I didn't mean to dump all that on you. Nothing drearier than someone complaining about her money problems. I hear it from my clients all the time when I'm trying to get them to pay their bills."

Russ felt lower than an armadillo's toes. "I wish you'd told me earlier about this." He'd had no idea she was in financial trouble. In fact, looking at her clothes, her car and her jewelry, he'd figured just the opposite.

"I don't want anyone feeling sorry for me, so stop it," she said, her voice severe. "Most of his debts are secured by the business, which means they can't touch his retirement fund, so he won't be out on the street or anything like that. We'll just get through it—"

"I could do more than offer sympathy. I could sign your contract."

It looked like she had stopped breathing for a moment. But then she shook her head. "I couldn't ask you to do that, especially after meeting Winnie. I'd be messing up two lives and there's no guarantee I could fix things for my dad even if I had the money to do it. You said it best—throwing money at a problem isn't always the answer. Maybe it's simply time for—"

"Sydney, stop. I've been a complete imbecile about this whole inheritance thing. Of course I'll sign the contract. I'll set up a trust with the money, like you said, and use it to pro-

tect the wilderness and the animals and clean up pollution—
I could do a lot of good things."

"But what about Winnie?"

"You let me worry about her. I'll just have to explain things
to her. I could fix it so she could get a small income, enough
that she'd never have to struggle but not enough to tempt
her beyond her capacity. And Bert. I could make sure Bert's
okay."

Sydney's eyes filled with tears again. "You'd be giving me
everything I said I wanted in the first place, but now I'd feel
guilty taking it."

"Where's the contract? I'll sign it right now. Is a million
dollars enough to save your father's business?"

"Way more than enough. Russ…are you sure? You were
so adamant before about—"

"I'm positive. You can get the contract now or give it to me
later, but I won't change my mind."

"Oh, Russ!" She threw her arms around him in an exuberant hug. "You have no idea—you just have no idea. My dad
will be so excited. Not about the money, but the bragging
rights. Everyone has tried to solve this case, for years and
years, and Baines & Baines will get the credit. It'll do won-
ders for business."

Yeah, well, he'd known he wouldn't be able to avoid pub-
licity. "Do me a favor, okay? Can you wait to tell anyone until
I've talked to Winnie? I want to break it to her gently that
we're not headed for *Lifestyles of the Rich and Famous*."

"Of course I will. Take as long as you need." She hugged
him again, but given the fact he was naked and she was almost, the proximity of their bodies led to more earthy results

than mere gratitude. He scooted her onto his lap, where she was not able to miss the fact he was fully aroused.

"You look better in my shirt than I do," he said just before kissing her.

There was no hesitation in her response. "It makes a dandy robe."

"You can use it any time." He reached inside the shirt and cupped her breasts, rubbing his thumbs over the nipples, and she shuddered. By signing her contract, it meant their business would not be concluded today. There would be details to attend to, probably all kinds of affidavits and government forms.

He would get to see her again.

"I know you have to go back to New York," he said as he kissed her neck. "But you'll come back to Texas, won't you?"

"You want me to?"

"God, yes."

"Because I was thinking," she said as she swiveled around to straddle him, "that I don't want this to be over. We're too good together."

Amen to that. Then they were beyond words as Russ lifted her hips and lowered her onto his arousal. She moaned with uninhibited pleasure as their sensual dance moved faster and faster, culminating in a shattering climax that sent them both hurtling into space.

When they returned to earth a few minutes later, Russ simply held Sydney in his arms and stroked her hair. Maybe she wasn't like all those other city girls. Maybe they had a future. If the past three days stuck in the woods hadn't scared her off, she wasn't easily scared. If he lost her, it would be because he'd screwed up. He wouldn't be able to blame it on the great outdoors.

"I need to get going," she said. "It's getting late and I still have to return my aunt's car."

"I know. Why don't you go shower and I'll fix you something for breakfast."

Russ whistled as he toasted a bagel and poured some orange juice. This was going to work out. Somehow, it would be okay. Winnie would understand. She might be mad at him for a while, but she'd changed since their Vegas days. She'd grown up along with him. Maybe he wasn't giving her enough credit and she would accept his decision without a fight.

When Sydney reappeared a few minutes later, she was wearing a black-and-white houndstooth skirt and a black turtleneck, along with black stockings and her black, pointy-toed shoes. She looked pure New York.

"You sure you don't want to wear the hiking boots?" Russ asked. "Your ankle is going to bother you in those high heels."

"I've committed enough fashion faux pas for this year," she said with a grin. She had a sheaf of wrinkled papers in her hand. "This was in my briefcase." It was the contract.

He gave the contract a glance and signed it.

"Russ, aren't you going to read it? Maybe have a lawyer look it over?"

"Why? I trust you."

"It's just always a good idea to— Never mind. I guess you're used to doing business on a handshake."

"Damn right," he said with a grin. "But with you, it was better than a handshake."

Sydney drank the orange juice and ate half a bagel, claiming she wasn't hungry after last night's decadent meal. And then it was time for her to leave.

She gathered up her things—her small suitcase, briefcase and purse. "I'll call you when I get home. Is that…is that okay?" She nibbled her lower lip uncertainly.

"While you were in the shower I programmed all three of my numbers—home, office and cell—into your phone." He handed her the phone, which she'd left on the sofa.

"Perfect. Walk me out?"

He'd like to walk her out, get into her car and go with her back to New York. "I've never been to New York," he said. "I should go some time."

She smiled. "I can guarantee you'll have a place to stay."

While Sydney threw her things in the BMW's backseat, Russ opened the garage door—and was greeted with a camera flash.

A man strode into the garage and shoved a microphone into Russ's face. "Russ Klein, how does it feel to be Texas's newest millionaire?"

Russ just stood there, too stunned to say anything. In his driveway was one TV news van, several other vehicles and a half-dozen strangers with cameras, microphones and lights, all of them focused on him.

He glanced over his shoulder at Sydney, who stood next to her car with her hand over her mouth, doing a pretty good imitation of shock.

Russ finally found his voice. "I have no comment," he said, "and please get off my property." With that he retreated into the garage and pushed the button to close the garage door. He didn't chance another look at Sydney until they were safely blocked from view.

She looked utterly befuddled.

"That didn't take you long," he said. "Did you call them from the phone in the bedroom while I was making breakfast?"

"Russ! I didn't call anyone."

"Well, I didn't tell anyone, so that leaves you."

"But I didn't—"

"Or maybe you planned this days ago, before I ever agreed to sign the contract. Maybe you thought if word got out, my mother would already know about the money, so I would no longer have any reason not to accept the money and give you your cut."

"I would never—"

"Is your father really near bankruptcy, or was that your last-ditch effort to appeal to my sympathy?" He knew he was being harsh, but the sense of betrayal he felt was overwhelming. He'd trusted Sydney. God help him, he'd fallen in love with her—or the woman he thought she was. But now he was beginning to see it was all a carefully orchestrated image designed to manipulate him where she wanted him to go.

"Do you really have any feelings for me?" he continued relentlessly. "Or was that all a lie, too? I notice you didn't mention anything about wanting to continue our relationship until I'd agreed to accept the money. Why settle for a measly ten percent when you could have access to all of it, if you played your cards right?"

She wasn't saying anything, he noticed. A moment ago she'd had denials ready to fling, but suddenly she'd gone quiet as a crypt. It was hard to tell, but her eyes looked suspiciously shiny as she eyed him, reminding him uncomfortably of a dog who'd been kicked and expected to be kicked again.

Without a word she turned back to her car, opened the passenger door and leaned inside, rummaging around in the backseat. What was she doing?

"Nothing to say for yourself?"

She straightened and handed him a sheaf of papers. "Here's the contract. We can pretend you never signed it. You can tell the reporters they've made a mistake."

"No, I gave my word and I never go back on a promise." Unlike some people.

"Fine." She ripped the contract in half, then into quarters, then once again, letting the pieces flutter to his garage floor like confetti. "I wouldn't take this commission even if I were homeless and starving." She marched around to the front of the car, still limping slightly, he couldn't help noticing.

Now it was his turn to stare, speechless, as she climbed into the BMW and slammed the door. She started the engine, immediately filling the closed space with exhaust. He had to open the door or asphyxiate them both.

Suddenly he didn't want to let her go. Why had she torn up the contract? It made no sense. Unless...

"Would you open the damn door?" she shouted through her open window.

He walked to the button and pushed it. The garage door roared open. The reporters had moved, but only as far as the street. They were still waiting for him like a pack of coyotes.

"Sydney, wait," he called to her. "Maybe we need to talk."

"You did enough talking for both of us," she yelled out the window, backing out like a contender in the demolition derby. "You already have all the answers. Hope your self-righteousness keeps you warm at night." Her window slid up and she hit the gas and flew down the driveway, gravel flying.

No, no, this wasn't right. Was it some new game she was playing? Why had she torn up the contract? But he didn't get the opportunity to find out, because she was heading down the driveway like a greased bullet. A couple of the media types tried to stop her, but they had to jump out of her way to avoid being run over because she wasn't stopping for anything.

Russ was left standing in his garage with a ripped-up contract, staring after her, wondering who'd been driving the freight train that had just wrecked his life. He suspected it might be himself.

## Chapter Fifteen

Sydney found her way to the main highway only by chance. She was so upset, so *furious,* she couldn't think straight, couldn't remember the twists and turns they'd taken last night to reach Russ's house. And even if she'd remembered the way, her eyes were so full of tears she couldn't read the street signs.

But instinct must have guided her, because she blundered onto Highway 350, which she knew would take her to Austin.

With one unfounded accusation, Russ had yanked off the wings she'd been soaring with, causing her to crash with a pain much worse than a sprained ankle. Had those days they spent together meant nothing to him? She'd have trusted him with her life and she *had* trusted him with feelings and secrets she'd never confessed to anyone.

Apparently he hadn't felt the same about her, because he didn't give it two seconds' thought. He'd seen those cameras and immediately assumed the woman he'd held in his arms all night long was a greedy liar with no conscience.

She had no idea how the media had found out about the story, but it sure as hell hadn't come from her.

She cried all the way to Austin, though she didn't want to

waste tears on someone who obviously thought so little of her, she couldn't seem to stop. She'd been so happy. For the first time since her mother's death she'd been hopeful about the future—her father's *and* her own.

When she pulled into her aunt Carol's covered parking space at her retirement villa, she used the visor mirror to try to repair the damage caused by her crying. But as soon as Aunt Carol opened the door to her apartment, she knew something was wrong.

"What in the world happened?" Carol said as she greeted Sydney with a warm hug that smelled of Cashmere Bouquet bath powder. The scent was comforting, almost maternal. Carol wore one of her signature silk pantsuits—she had them in every color under the sun—her makeup perfect, her bright red hair salon fresh.

"It's a man, of course," Sydney said. "What else?" Aunt Carol was twice divorced, so that was a sentiment she could relate to.

"Ooooh, men. It's too bad we need them to procreate, otherwise I'd say let's do away with the entire gender. Come in and tell me about it, sweetheart. I'll fix you some hot tea and toast with marmalade."

Sydney smiled. Carol had been offering her special brand of comfort for as long as Sydney could remember. Though they didn't see each other more than once or twice a year, Aunt Carol, herself childless, had always made her only niece feel special.

"I really need to get to the airport," Sydney said. "I've got a flight out at ten-thirty-something."

"I'll drive you," Carol offered. "You can tell me about it on the way."

Sydney didn't really want to talk about this yet. It was too raw, like a freshly skinned knee. But Aunt Carol insisted, so she told the whole story, beginning to end.

"If you didn't alert the media, who did?" Carol asked.

Sydney shook her head. "Unless some other investigator was following my tracks. You don't suppose Dad…"

"No, I talked to him this morning. He doesn't know anything."

"He will—probably by the time I get back to New York he'll have heard. And I'll have to confess to him that I tore up the contract."

Carol clicked her tongue. "You shouldn't have done that. A million dollars could make up for a lot of heartbreak." Carol would know, since both of her ex-husbands had left her pretty well-set.

"I couldn't have Russ Klein believing I would sell him out like that!"

"Do you think your gesture did the job? Do you think he believes you didn't sic the reporters on him?"

"I don't know. And I don't care. He could crawl back to me on hands and knees begging forgiveness, and I wouldn't even consider it. Who wants a man who would jump to conclusions based on such flimsy evidence?"

"What else was he supposed to think?"

That stopped Sydney cold. "You're taking his side?"

"Granted, he shouldn't have accused you without giving you a chance to explain or plead your case, but—"

"I can't believe you think he has a leg to stand on! He was horrid."

"Men are horrid in general," Carol agreed. "Anyone who claims women are the emotional ones have never seen a man jumping to conclusions and defending his reasons for doing so. But sooner or later he's going to realize he made a mistake. Then you'll know whether he has real character or not. If he can admit he was wrong, if he can apologize, if he can learn from his mistakes, he might be worth a second look."

"Hmph," Sydney sniffed. "Not in a million years. He had his chance. We had real potential and he blew it."

"He's only known you a few days. Mind-blowing sex is a great start, but it's hard to trust someone you've known such a short time, especially in the face of damning evidence."

"Forget it. It's over. I'm going to confess everything to Dad, then we're going to file for bankruptcy and I'll pick up the pieces." Somehow.

"I'll say one more thing, than I'll shut up."

"Okay, what?"

"Don't be too hasty."

"I'm not the one who was hasty."

RUSS HAD TO GO INTO THE STORE. Bert had been kind enough to cover for him the past couple of days, but today a party of six were coming in to get outfitted for a hunting trip. Russ didn't sell guns, but he sold just about everything else and he needed to be there when his customers arrived.

Most of the reporters had gone away by nine o'clock, when Russ was ready to leave his house, but one enterprising young man remained. Russ stopped at the end of his driveway and rolled down the window, reassured by the fact that no cameras were visible.

"Mr. Klein? I'm Dewey Thompson from the *Austin*—"

"Just hold your horses," Russ interrupted him. "I'm saying one thing and one thing only to the press, so get it right, okay?"

"Um, okay," the reporter said uncertainly.

"I am not a millionaire and I have no intention of becoming one."

"But…but, Mr. Klein—"

Russ rolled up his window and headed into town. He parked down the street from the general store, then turned the collar up on his jacket and pulled down his hat as he made his way down the alley to the store's back door.

Bert met him almost before he got the door open. "What in tarnation is going on? I got reporters settin' on the sidewalk out front just lickin' their lips waiting for nine-thirty so I'll open the doors. I told 'em you weren't here, but they don't care. Apparently they want to come in and take pictures of your store, with or without you. Is it true? Did you really inherit ten million dollars?"

This was nuts. He wouldn't have been surprised if one or two reporters had been interested in interviewing him. It's not every day a long-lost heir finds out his estranged father left him ten million dollars and Sammy Oberlin had been a minor celebrity, at least in certain circles. But the media attention was way out of proportion, the type of frenzy reserved for rock stars, NFL quarterbacks and Tom Cruise.

"I *could* inherit the money," Russ said as he closed and locked the back door behind him, "but I'm choosing not to. I don't want to be rich."

"Boy, are you touched in the head?"

"I got my reasons."

"This has something to do with the city girl, I'll bet. I knew she was trouble the minute I laid eyes on her."

"Yeah, me, too." Thinking about Sydney made his heart ache, and he couldn't escape the suspicion that things weren't exactly as they seemed.

What was he going to do? He couldn't conduct business with reporters camped out on the sidewalk or prowling his store. Telling them they were mistaken would just fuel the fire. They could do their own research and verify he was Sammy Oberlin's son. If he told them he wasn't accepting the money, it would become an even bigger story.

And Winnie. Dear God, he had to talk to his mother before she saw all the cameras. Staying concealed in the back storage room, Russ took out his cell phone to call his mother. Maybe he could arrange to meet her someplace away from prying eyes, where he could break the news to her gently.

He already had three messages. He ran through them quickly, praying one would be from Sydney, but all three were from Winnie, wanting to know why he wouldn't answer his phone. He started to call her back when he heard the front door open.

Winnie. It had to be. She was the only other person who had a key besides Bert and Russ himself.

"Russ? Yoo-hoo, sweetie, are you here? I saw your car parked down the street."

Russ emerged from the storeroom and Winnie trotted across the wood floor in her high heels, her arms outstretched. "I can't believe you kept this all a secret from me!"

Russ allowed himself to be swallowed by his mother's exuberant hug. He hugged her back; this might be the last time she hugged him for a while. Winnie was generous with her affection, but she had a powerful temper and when she was mad at him she would sometimes refuse to talk to him for days.

"This just blows my mind," Winnie said as she released him. "Sammy hardly ever even looked at you. He must have found a conscience in his old age, 'cause he sure as heck didn't have one when I knew him."

"Mom, we have to talk."

"We will, honey, we will. But those reporters are the ones you ought to talk to right now. You've got to get used to being in the public eye, 'cause you're going to be an important man." She giggled like a schoolgirl. "My son, the multimillionaire."

"No, Mom, you don't have all the—"

"You'll look handsome on TV." She straightened his collar and then spit on her hand to smooth down his hair like she'd done when he was a little boy.

"I'm not talking to the reporters and that's final. And you shouldn't talk to them, either."

"Why in heaven's name not? They seem like nice enough fellas." Winnie strolled to the coffeepot and poured herself a cup. As usual, when she had an idea in her head, she didn't listen to anyone. "The first thing I'm going to buy is a new coat. I know it's hardly ever cold enough down here to wear fur, but I sure could have used one these last few days. Which do you think is better, mink or chinchilla? Or maybe fox?"

"None of the above. Mom—"

"Oh, that's right, you like all the furry little critters. And what do men know about fur coats, anyway? Oh, gosh, I'm just so excited I can't hardly think straight. I don't know how I'm going to fix people's hair today without making everybody turn out like Ozzy Osbourne. Do you think I should keep working? I love the Cut 'n' Curl, but it does tie me down and I've always wanted to travel. Where's the first place we should go? Paris? Or maybe Rio."

Russ was worn out just listening to her. He shook his head and got his own coffee. Maybe she'd wind down in a few minutes and let him get a word in edgewise. Until then, it was useless to try to interrupt.

"Where's Sydney, anyway?" she asked abruptly.

He waited to see if Winnie would pause long enough to allow him to answer. She took a long sip of her coffee, frowning at him over the rim of her cup.

"She went back to New York," he said, amazed Winnie had let him finish a sentence.

"I like her. I wasn't sure if she would even be nice to me after you said she was a stalker. But when she came into the Cut 'n' Curl dressed down in jeans and a flannel shirt—well, she looked like she belonged in Linhart and she was nice as pie."

Russ turned away. He didn't want to think about Sydney, dressed in his old clothes a mile too big for her and still looking sexy as hell.

"And she was so easy to talk to. I hope she lets me do her hair some time. She's got gorgeous hair. Did you say she went back to New York?"

Russ nodded.

"But she's coming back here, right? To settle everything. How long will it take, do you think, before they give you the money? I'm sure there are all kinds of legal requirements and, of course, Uncle Sam has to take his cut, but that still leaves an awful lot."

"I'm not accepting the money."

Winnie laughed. "Russ, don't be silly. You do love to tease your mama." She shook her head, still chuckling. "Not accepting the money, that's a good one."

"I'm not teasing," he said. "I don't want the money."

But she didn't seem to hear him. "I have to go open up the salon, I've got an appointment first thing with Eleanor Ivans. She's the one, you know, who always wants to compare the size of her diamonds with other people's. I can't wait to buy something that'll make her faint dead away! Oh, and Russ, think about talking to the reporters," she said with a pout. "They'll just keep pestering you until you give them what they want."

She drained her coffee cup and set it down. "Thanks for the coffee, sweetie. I'll see you later—we have to do something special to celebrate. Bert, you can come with us!"

Bert mumbled something about watching the Titanic sink and made his way to his rocking chair by the stove. Nero followed him, keeping a wary eye on Winnie, who was heading for the door, still talking. She exited with the same drama as she entered, in a cloud of perfume.

"Are you always this effective dealing with your mama?" Bert asked.

THE TRIP HOME was miserable. In her haze of despair, Sydney had forgotten to check her purse, and her tiny bottle of Vera Wang perfume got confiscated at security. No doubt that mean-faced witch of a security guard now smelled terrific.

The flight was delayed—it seemed the airline industry still hadn't fully recovered from the erratic weather patterns that had brought airports all over the country to a standstill. The plane, once it finally got in the air, was full of screaming toddlers. Worse, the man sitting next to Sydney was some kind of germophobe who obviously thought her intermittent sniffling meant she had a terrible cold. He tried to crawl out the window every time she pulled a tissue from her purse.

The taxi line at LaGuardia was twenty people deep, so when Sydney finally, finally made it home to her apartment, she was so exhausted all she wanted to do was sleep for a week. Her ankle was throbbing again. Seemed she would be stuck with that little souvenir of her trip to Texas for a long time to come.

She couldn't afford to hibernate. She had hundreds of e-mails to cull—and an anxious father to deal with. With dread weighing heavy on her, she called him at home. And when he didn't answer, she tried the office, though at four in the afternoon she doubted he would be there.

He surprised her by answering, sounding far more upbeat than he had in weeks.

"Dad?"

"Sweetheart! How is my champion heir-finder?"

Uh-oh. "What have you heard?"

"Only that my smart and talented daughter located the Oberlin heir when no one else could, not even her smart and talented old man. Why didn't you tell me you were onto this? I could have helped you out, not that you needed any help. I'm so proud, I've had to sew the buttons back on my shirt three times."

This was going to be way harder than she'd thought. Because as proud as he was of her now, that was as disappointed as he was going to be when he found out she blew it. No million-dollar commission. With her luck, some other heir-finder would harass Russ until he signed a contract just to get rid of them.

"Dad, you don't have the whole story," she said quickly. "I think some of what you've heard might be premature. I'll meet you at the office and we can talk about it there, okay?"

"Okay, but then we're going out to dinner to celebrate. Someplace expensive—I'm tired of pinching pennies."

Sydney didn't worry about changing clothes for a fancy dinner. It would never happen, once she confessed everything to Lowell. She threw on a pair of jeans, a Mets sweatshirt and a ratty pair of running shoes. Her hair was a disaster, so she pulled it back into a ponytail. When she inspected herself in the mirror, she decided she looked ill.

Maybe Lowell would feel sorry for her.

Consistent with her recent spate of luck, she couldn't get a cab, so despite the sore ankle she hoofed it to the office building that housed Baines & Baines. It was only a few blocks away.

The office building that housed Baines & Baines had retail space on the street level. One of the stores was a pet shop. Normally Sydney passed it without a second glance. But today, something in the window caught her attention.

It was Nero. Or rather, a puppy version of Nero. As she gazed in the window, the bloodhound puppy jumped to its big, clumsy feet and pressed its wet nose against the glass, wagging its long tail as if it had just spotted a long-lost friend.

Russ was right about one thing. She didn't really dislike dogs, she was afraid of them. But this puppy with the huge feet and liquid brown eyes plucked at her heartstrings. In Linhart, she hadn't wanted to admit it, but Russ's devotion to the old dog had been part of his appeal.

A sign in the window announced that the price on the dog had been reduced, probably because it was getting too big and eating the pet shop out of any hope for a profit.

On impulse, Sydney walked into the store and buttonholed an employee. "I want to look at that bloodhound in the window, please."

The young man smiled. "She's a charmer, isn't she?" He went to the window to retrieve the pooch while Sydney just stood there, wondering if she was losing her mind.

"Her name's Blossom. Of course, you can change it." The

moment the employee set the dog on the floor, it galumphed over to Sydney and began sniffing her shoe, just as Nero had.

Sydney sat down on the floor and the puppy was all over her, sniffing and licking, grabbing the hem of her sweatshirt and tugging, grabbing her shoelaces in her sharp little teeth.

"She's fifteen weeks and getting too big for the shop. If we don't sell her soon…" He let his voice trail off meaningfully. "She's a full-blooded bloodhound but she doesn't have any papers, so the owner's willing to let her go cheap."

Sydney reached into her purse and withdrew her credit card. "Ring her up. And throw in a bag of food."

"Um, you'll need some other stuff, too," the eager employee said, probably spotting a sucker when he saw one. "Do you have a carrier? Collar and leash? You'll want to get a tag, too, in case she gets lost."

Sydney had the dog in her arms and was pressing her face into the soft brown fur. The puppy even smelled a little bit like Nero. She never thought she would like the smell of dog.

"Just the food for now—and a collar and leash," she amended, because Blossom would have to be walked. "Gather up all the other stuff I'll need and I'll be back tomorrow to get it, okay?"

"Sure," the young man said. "You won't be sorry. Blossom's an awesome dog."

Minutes later, Sydney was the proud owner of an unregistered bloodhound that would have to be walked several times a day. She lived in a building that didn't allow pets. This was going to be interesting.

The security guard at her father's building looked askance as she entered with the dog in her arms, but she'd given him a nice Christmas gift, so he was inclined to look the other way.

She took the elevator to the fourth floor and braced for what was likely to be a very unpleasant conversation.

The offices of Baines & Baines were small and humble, only a couple of rooms. Theirs wasn't the kind of business that got a lot of foot traffic, so there was no need for anything fancy.

Lowell sat at one of the two desks in the front office he used to share with Shirley. It appeared he'd tidied up the place while Sydney was gone, which was a small miracle. He hadn't so much as opened a file drawer in months.

He turned to her with a big dirt-eating grin. "There's my star— Holy cow, what have you got there?"

"Um, a dog?"

"I thought you were afraid of dogs."

"I'm not a dog person," she corrected him. "This is a puppy, though."

"Yeah, but it'll grow into a dog. Where'd it come from?"

"I just bought her. It's all part of my new campaign."

"You mean, like advertising?" Lowell asked, obviously confused. "Hey, having a bloodhound as our logo could work. Maybe we could do a TV commercial! We'll have the money to do more promotion now."

"Um, yeah. Dad, we need to talk." She set Blossom on the floor and opened the bag of food. She hadn't purchased any food bowls, so she put some kibble in an empty coffee cup and set it on the floor. The puppy promptly tipped the mug over, spilling food everywhere, and started snuffling it up.

"You don't look like a woman who just earned herself a million dollars."

"Like I said on the phone, you don't quite have all the facts." She walked over to the other desk, swiveled the chair around and sat, weary to the bone. "I did find the Oberlin heir. It was a complete accident and I wasn't sure I was right, so I didn't tell you because I didn't want to get your hopes up."

"But you found him, right? This Russell Klein?"

Sydney sighed. "Yeah. He's the one. But I don't have a signed contract. He did sign a contract, but then I got mad at him and tore it up."

Lowell's jaw dropped. "Is this some kind of joke?"

"No. You did not raise a brilliant daughter. You raised an idiot."

"Wait a minute. Don't tell me…this is the guy? *The* guy you told me about last night on the phone?"

"'Fraid so. But he accused me of lying and betraying him when I'd gone out of my way to be understanding about his situation."

"What exactly is his situation?" Lowell wanted to know.

So she told him about Russ's childhood and Winnie and how he'd built a really happy life down in Texas and didn't want to wreck it. "But then he realized it was dumb not to accept the money and he did it. He did it for me, because he knew how badly we needed this commission."

"Honey, you did him a favor. Not the other way around."

She'd figured Lowell wouldn't understand. Sydney herself had struggled to comprehend why Russ had refused the money. It was only when she spent time in Linhart and experienced the charms of small-town life herself—and met Winnie—that she'd started to understand.

"At any rate, he asked me not to tell anyone I'd found the Oberlin heir until he'd talked to his mother and explained he was putting the money into a trust. And, of course, I agreed; no harm in that. But somehow the media found out."

"And he thought you were responsible?" Lowell asked, managing to muster up some righteous indignation of his own. "He called you a liar?"

"Pretty much, yeah."

"I got news for that deluded young man. He might be trying to protect his mama, but she's the one who alerted the media."

That caught Sydney up short. "Winnie Klein? Are you sure?"

"I saw her on CNN. Nice-lookin' gal with big blond hair and a bust measurement about the same as her IQ?"

"Dad, that's not very nice." Sydney felt compelled to defend Winnie. "She must not be too dumb, because she sure put two and two together." And Sydney wished she could be there when Russ found out.

"So you're telling me there's no million-dollar commission?" Lowell said, finally grasping the most significant point of this conversation.

She nodded miserably. "I let my pride get in the way of common sense. Sorry, Dad."

He reached over and squeezed her knee. "That's okay, darlin'. I'm still proud of you. I wish you'd come work with me full-time. As a partner, a full partner."

"Really? You mean it?"

"You're every inch your mother. You know, sometimes she refused a commission when she thought the client needed it more than us. Nothing wrong with letting your emotions rule once in a while."

Sydney expelled a long breath of air. "We're going to have to declare bankruptcy."

Lowell winced. "Guess I saw that coming."

## Chapter Sixteen

Russ somehow managed to get through the day. He got the hunting party outfitted in all the latest gear, garnering a nice profit. Of course, he wouldn't have to worry about how profitable the store was if he accepted the ten million bucks.

Around noon the reporters gave up on him. They'd shot a few photos of him, but when he refused to be interviewed, they'd wandered off to greener stories.

For the remainder of the afternoon, the store was besieged by a string of customers who'd come in pretending to shop so they could gawk at him—or to offer sincere congratulations, because of course most normal people would see a windfall like this as good fortune. In fact, Russ was probably the only person in the world who saw it as a curse.

Sydney had brought a curse down on him, that was all there was to it. But whatever anger he'd felt toward her had dissipated during the day. He kept thinking about how she'd torn up the contract. If her only motive was money, she would never have done that. He couldn't escape the niggling doubt that he'd somehow gotten it all wrong.

But Sydney *had* to be the one who'd alerted the media. Or

at the very least, she'd told someone who then contacted the press. Which meant she'd lied. She'd manipulated him in the name of blatant self-interest; therefore she wasn't the sort of person he wanted to be involved with romantically or do business with.

Bert had been fielding calls all day on his cell phone. He and his network of gossipers had kept the airwaves humming, though Bert was doing his best to quell the worst of the rumors.

Late in the afternoon, he hung up from a call looking troubled. "That was Eleanor Ivans. She said Winnie's been up and down Main Street shopping, and she just bought a diamond necklace."

"What?" Russ cursed softly. He'd wanted to wait until some of Winnie's giddy excitement had worn off before sitting her down and forcing her to believe him when he said he wasn't taking the money. But he couldn't wait if she was running up her credit cards.

He shoved his sleeves into his jacket. "I'll be back."

"Dang, I'd like to be a fly on the wall for this conversation," Bert said unhelpfully.

Russ found Winnie still in Stover's Fine Jewelry. She smiled a greeting, but her smile faded when Russ scowled at her. She was wearing the necklace, which was so heavy with diamonds he was surprised she could stand up straight.

"Mom, what do you think you're doing?"

"Just a little shopping. I haven't had any sparklies since I sold the ones Sammy gave me and I didn't think you'd mind."

"I do mind. Return the necklace. Now. Then you and I are going to have a little chat."

"I don't see what you're getting all bent out of shape for. I was gonna put it on layaway 'cause I know how you hate it when I run up my credit cards. But you'll buy it for me, won't you? It would just be a drop in the bucket."

He hated it when Winnie used that little-girl voice with him. He thought she'd outgrown it. "Just give the necklace back to the nice man. Then we'll go back to the Cut 'n' Curl and go into your office and I'm going to talk and you're going to listen."

Winnie looked perturbed, but she unfastened the necklace and handed it back to the patient Mr. Stover. "Don't sell it to anyone else, Arthur, please?"

"I'll put your name on it."

She winked at the elderly jeweler, then followed Russ outside and down the street to the beauty shop, holding her head high and walking like a queen.

Betty and Glory, who both had customers, stopped what they were doing to applaud Russ when he entered.

"Afternoon, ladies," he said, hating the attention. He wasn't crazy; this was proving he'd been right all along. Being rich would be nothing but a pain in the butt. He escorted Winnie into the small office in the back where she kept her books, did the payroll, placed hair-product orders and paid bills. She'd proved herself surprisingly competent at running her business. But for some reason, that expertise did not extend to her personal finances.

Travel magazines and brochures for cruises and safaris were spread out all over her desk. "You haven't ordered anything else, have you? You haven't booked any luxury vacations or bought a Mercedes or anything like that?"

"No, but if we're going to be rich, I don't see what the problem is. Do you have any idea how much money ten million dollars is? We couldn't spend it in a lifetime if we tried."

Winnie could. That woman could spend it in a year. But

it was a moot point, because there wouldn't be any money to spend.

"I'm going to talk and you're going to listen. Okay?"

She nodded, looking a little scared.

"Sammy did, indeed, leave me a pile of money. But I'm not going to accept it."

"Excuse me?"

He held up his finger. "I'm talking, remember?"

"But I'm not hearing right."

"Mom, have you been happy? Since we moved to Linhart, I mean. Just nod."

She nodded.

"And you love the Cut 'n' Curl. You said when you were a little girl you always wanted your own beauty parlor. And when you bought it, you said it was a dream come true."

She nodded again.

"We have good friends here, right? People who love us for who we are, not for what we can buy them."

Another nod.

"Now, do you remember what life was like in Vegas? Parties, booze, drugs, people mooching off you. Sleeping till noon, waking with a hangover. Begging for money from Sammy, then spending it like water with nothing to show for it."

She stared at the wall behind Russ, remembering.

"I'm not saying money is bad," he continued. "But you and I weren't meant to be rich. I love my life. And you love yours. Having a bunch of money would just mess things up."

Winnie grabbed a tissue from a box on the desk and dabbed at her eyes.

"You can talk now."

"You're really going to refuse it?"

"Yes."

"Well, crap. If I'd known that, I never would have called CNN and the *Enquirer.*"

Russ suddenly felt like he couldn't get enough air. The room tilted and he grabbed on to the arms of his chair. "You called the media?"

"When you inherit millions from a notorious Las Vegas mobster, it's not the kind of thing you want to keep a secret. I always wanted to be in the *Enquirer,* you know that. Not for something gross, like a hundred-pound tumor, but for something cool."

"So Sydney told you about Sammy's will," he concluded.

"Oh, no, she never breathed a word about it. In fact, she never even mentioned what kind of work she did. But Bert knew some of it and that was enough to get me started. I looked her up on the Internet. Said she was an heir-finder. Then Betty's son, the lawyer, explained what an heir-finder was. I was dying to know what business she had with you, so Betty and I did some more Googling. Did you know there's a whole Web site devoted to finding you?"

Russ's gut clenched so tight, he thought he might lose his lunch. What had he done? How could he have been so stupid?

"Russ, sweetie, you don't look so good. Your face has gone white and you're all pinched around the mouth. Want me to get you a Diet Coke? It's all I have in the fridge."

"No, thanks." When he was pretty sure he could stand without passing out, he did. "I'm sorry for all the confusion."

"I guess I should have waited to talk to you before I started counting my chickens, huh?"

"In retrospect, that might have been the wiser choice, but it's okay."

"Are you mad at me?"

"I thought you'd be mad at *me*."

"No. I think you're a chucklehead for walking away from that kind of money, but I'm not mad. Just disappointed. I really wanted that necklace."

"They're just rocks, Mom."

She rolled her eyes. "Sometimes I wonder how we could be related."

Back on Main Street, Russ inhaled deeply. He had to call Sydney and apologize. No, an apology wasn't going to do it. He was going to have to grovel. When he remembered the things he'd said to her that morning, he cringed.

His mother was right; he was a chucklehead.

He didn't even wait until he got back to the store. He used his cell to dial hers. But he only got her voice mail.

"Sydney, it's Russ. I'm sorry. I'm just so, so sorry and I was completely wrong and deluded and a total ass…" He couldn't think of any other good groveling sentiments off the top of his head, so he ended with, "Please call me."

He doubted she would. Sydney was the best thing ever to happen to him, way better than ten million dollars, and he'd foolishly driven her away. If he'd been Sydney, he would have told himself to go to hell.

SYDNEY WAS FINALLY ABLE to see the top of her desk in her home office. She'd spent most of the day dealing with her own clients, putting out fires and responding to potential new customers who'd contacted her during her absence. Most of them had gone elsewhere for their security needs, but she'd made a couple of appointments.

She'd also spent a lot of time taking Blossom for walks, carefully dodging her apartment manager. But she was going to have to move if she wanted to keep the dog. And dammit, she was keeping the stupid dog, which had cried all night until Sydney had brought her into bed with her. Now they had bonded.

She had to keep her eye on the puppy every minute. She'd already destroyed one house slipper, one table leg and the corner of her bedspread.

But as infuriating as the puppy was, she was so darn cute and lovable, Sydney couldn't even consider finding her another home. The dog was hers, for better or worse. And if every time Sydney looked at the dog she was reminded of Nero and then Russ, that was just too bad. Maybe she wouldn't open herself up so easily to the next broad-shouldered good ol' boy who pretended to have all kinds of values and morals and ethics, but who could so easily assume she was a slime bucket.

She didn't fault him for suspecting her. But he could have investigated before throwing accusations at her. She still fumed every time she thought of how easily he'd dismissed the bond they'd forged. And accusing her of making up the story about her poor grieving father's nearly bankrupt business—how could he believe *anyone* would do that, much less the woman he'd just spent all night making love to?

Her cell phone rang, and she checked the caller ID: Russ again. He'd been leaving voice mail messages every couple of hours all day long and the previous evening, too.

Sydney couldn't talk to him yet. Her feelings were too raw, too exposed. But she kept listening to the voice mails just to hear the sound of his voice and remember what it was like to be in love, if only briefly.

"Sydney, I'm searching for your office but I can't find it. I'm standing out on the corner of Atlantic and Court streets looking like an idiot. Someone handed me a dollar because they thought I was homeless. Please help."

Russ was here? In Brooklyn? The man she'd firmly believed would never set foot outside central Texas had gotten on a plane and flown to the biggest, most crowded city in America to see her?

She went to her window and looked out. *Oh, my God.* There he was, standing across the street by Your Personal Assistant, Inc., which was a mailbox and secretarial service. After a stalking incident a couple of years back, she didn't give out her physical address to people she didn't know. The address on her business card was the one Russ had found.

Her heart ached as she looked at him, so out of place with his cowboy hat and his jeans and boots.

She decided to take pity on him. She would direct him to her office, accept his apology and send him back to Texas where he clearly belonged. She dialed the number, and he answered instantly.

"Sydney?"

"I can see you from my window. Cross the street. Turn right and come in the second doorway. I'll buzz you up. Take the elevator to the third floor." She disconnected and watched as he followed her directions.

When he got off the elevator, she was standing in the hallway, waiting for him, her arms folded. She didn't intend to make this easy for him. But then she realized she'd already made it pretty hard. He'd come all the way to New York just to see her.

"I was wrong," he said.

"Wow, that's a news flash."

"I made a mistake."

"You blew it, big-time. Do you know I was actually thinking about moving to Texas? That's how crazy I am—was—about you."

"You don't have to move. I could live here. New Yorkers probably need outdoor adventures in the worst way. I could do tours of the Hudson River and, uh, sewer explorations or something."

"Don't be ridiculous. You would never move to New York."

"If that's what it takes to be with you, Sydney, then, yes, I would. Not only yes, but hell, yes. Who cares about where you live? It's how you live and who you live with that matter."

She studied him, amazed at the lengths he was going to. Was it possible? Could he really care for her that much?

"You just don't like it that I was the one to walk away." She was grasping here, because he was getting to her. She'd sworn she would never speak to him again, that his name was no longer a part of her vocabulary. Yet here she was, standing a few feet from him, having to focus hard on not closing the distance between them and throwing herself against him, pressing her nose into his ubiquitous flannel shirt and inhaling that wonderful, manly male smell that was his and no one else's.

"You didn't walk away," he argued. "I drove you away. I knew I'd made a mistake before your car cleared the garage. If you really don't have any interest in seeing me, that's one thing. But if you're angry and hurt that I didn't trust you—and you have every right to be—there might be a chance you'll get over it."

"In fifty years," she shot back, folding her arms. "Or a hundred."

"That mad, huh?"

"It's not just that I'm mad. I...I..."

The elevator doors opened and a cleaning woman emerged with her cart and a vacuum cleaner. Giving Sydney and Russ a curt nod, she plugged in the vacuum cleaner and proceeded to clean the hall carpet.

Obviously they couldn't continue this conversation here in the hallway. Reluctantly, Sydney turned and led Russ down to her apartment. The moment Russ entered her home, a streak of brown fur went straight for him. Blossom bounced on her hind legs, then rebounded off Russ's knee and circled around in a dance of puppy joy. *Oh, boy, a new friend.*

"What is this?" Russ went down to the floor in a heartbeat, welcoming the exuberant puppy into his arms. She bathed his face in dog kisses.

"She needed a home," Sydney said, cross that she'd been found out.

"You don't like dogs," Russ said, laughing as he tried to push the puppy away. It was like pushing the ocean.

"Do you wonder why? She's the stupidest, most badly behaved animal on the planet." Sydney sat on the arm of her sofa, defeated. "She would have ended up at the animal shelter if I hadn't bought her. I was perfectly happy without a dog."

Russ scratched Blossom behind the ears and amazingly she calmed down. "She looks just like Nero did when he was a pup. Are you going to keep her?"

"You want her? She's yours." Of course, she didn't mean it.

"Okay. But I suspect if she comes, you'll come with her. You're crazy about this dog, I can tell."

This conversation wasn't going at all how Sydney thought it would. She hadn't expected to be tempted. She had naively believed that seeing Russ face to face she could banish him once and for all from her thoughts, shut off the memories in a closed file in her mind and get on with her life.

"I can't be with a man who's going to think the worst of me at every opportunity. I can't be with a man who doubts me, who has no faith in me. I'm not going to live my life trying to prove my loyalty. If I'm late for a date, will you assume I've been with another man? If I have a friendly chat with the grocery check boy, will you call it flirting? Will you be checking my pockets for notes from secret lovers, checking out my cell phone to see who I've been talking to?"

"I'm not like that," he said, standing up and giving Blossom one last pat. "I'm not normally jealous or suspicious. I'm very laid-back."

"What I saw yesterday morning was not laid-back."

"It was an isolated incident. I was shocked by those reporters. You'd been talking on the phone earlier, kind of secretive in the middle of the night, and I put two and two together and came up with five hundred. It won't happen again, I swear it. Just give me another chance. You can put me on probation."

How was she supposed to say no to that? She was willing to bet this man didn't humble himself very often. When she said nothing, because she was too busy hyperventilating, he kept going. She suspected he would keep talking until he convinced her or she kicked him out.

"I know we haven't known each other very long, but I'm thinking you're the one I want to be with the rest of my life. Sometimes a man just knows when something is right. I knew when I saw Linhart for the first time that I wanted to live there forever. I knew when Bert offered to sell me the general store that it was meant to be. And I knew when I held you in my arms when we were dancing, and even more when I kissed you, we had something special together. What I'm trying to say is that I love you."

Sydney blinked back tears. Was this really happening?

Blossom was busy gnawing on Russ's cowboy boots. Russ shook his foot, trying to dislodge the puppy. "Do you know how hard it is to declare your love with a dog attached to your shoe? C'mon, puppy, don't take away whatever small amount of dignity I might have left."

Sydney had run out of resistance. How could she not forgive a man with a puppy attached to his shoe? "I love you, too, you know? Despite my best efforts."

His sexy mouth started to widen into a grin, but he stopped it. "Is there a *but?* As in, 'but I could never spend my life with you'?"

She shook her head. "Can I kiss you now?"

"Um, Blossom beat you to it. Would you settle for a really good hug?"

She held out her arms. In a flash Russ had her in his embrace. He hugged her long and hard. "I was so afraid I'd never get to do this again. I mean it about moving to New York, too. There's no law that says you have to be the one to disrupt your life and I would never ask you to move away from your father when he needs you, or your job, since you love it."

"I don't care where we live. Just so we're together." She could do her kind of work anywhere as long as she wasn't too far from a city. Austin would do. She would move to Texas in a heartbeat if not for her father. But they could figure out something, she was sure of it.

The phone in her office rang. She considered ignoring it, but she wasn't really in a good position to turn down work.

Russ loosened his hold on her enough that she could slip into her office and grab the phone. "Baines Security."

"Wade Clancy returning your call."

Oh, hell. The bankruptcy lawyer. She refused to let that reminder dampen her happiness. It was just money. She made an appointment for the following afternoon, then wrote down the list of things she would need to bring with her—financial statements, tax returns and such.

Russ played with Blossom while Sydney conducted business. He loved how cool and efficient she was on the phone. No one talking to her would guess the passion that lay just beneath the surface.

He didn't mean to eavesdrop, but he couldn't help hearing part of her conversation, and he realized she was talking to someone about bankruptcy. Oh, hell, he couldn't let her do that. He'd forgotten his most important reason for coming here. Well, second-most important, after making up with Sydney. He reached into his jacket pocket and pulled out a rumpled and oddly contoured stack of papers. He waited until Sydney hung up, then wordlessly handed it to her.

"You're taking this back—no arguments."

She looked at the contract, then burst out laughing. "How long did it take you to Scotch-tape this back together?"

"Only a couple of hours."

Then she sobered. "Russ, are you sure?"

"I've already talked to my mom and she took the news far better than I would have expected. I told her I would set up retirement funds for both of us and for Bert, so we don't have to worry in our old age, but the rest is going to the Wildlife Preservation Cooperative, earmarked to buy land in the Hill Country and designate it a protected wilderness area. She thinks I need to see a psychiatrist, maybe a whole team of them, but she'll adjust to the idea. So you can just call that bankruptcy lawyer and cancel your appointment."

"You're a strange but generous man."

"The gesture is completely selfish. I want to raise my kids in a place that still has unspoiled woods and meadows and rivers and lakes. I don't want Bert's cabin to end up surrounded by ugly housing developments with cookie-cutter minimansions and no trees."

Sydney reached for her coat. "C'mon, let's go. I want you to meet someone."

"Your father?"

She nodded. "Don't be put off if he doesn't give you the warmest of receptions. We spent yesterday evening eating tempura, getting tipsy on saki and trashing you. But he'll warm up when he sees the contract."

They put on coats, then walked the seven blocks to her father's building, their gloved hands clasped. Blossom was on her leash, her behavior impossible. She charged at every person she saw wanting to make friends, wound her leash around Sydney's legs every thirty seconds or so, and generally made a nuisance of herself.

"Nero's going to love her," Russ said with a laugh as Sydney unwrapped the leash from a lamppost. "She needs obedience training, though."

"It's on my list."

They passed a jewelry store, and Russ stopped and looked in the window. "Let's go in here."

Sydney hesitated at the door.

"I need to buy my mother a peace offering," Russ said. "She wants a diamond necklace bigger than the one her friend

Eleanor has, and I figure I can unbend my principles enough to do that one thing for her. You can help me pick it out."

"Oh, okay."

"But you might look at engagement rings, too."

For a moment, she had that deer-in-headlights look and he worried that he'd pushed for too much. But he couldn't help it. He wanted no secrets between them, so she should know just exactly how serious his intentions were.

"If that was a marriage proposal, it lacked a certain something," she said with a nervous giggle. She looked absolutely adorable, standing there with the dog's leash wrapped around her once again.

"If I were to do a better job of it, would you say yes?"

She nodded without hesitation.

"Okay, just checking."

Thirty minutes later, Russ left the store with a necklace in his pocket that was even more spectacular than the one Winnie had picked out at Stover's. He also had a pretty good idea what type of diamond ring Sydney would like. He would buy that later and give it to her while on one knee in some appropriately romantic place, since that was what she wanted. But right now he was content with the fact that he and Sydney were together. Wherever they ended up, it would be home, because it would be filled with love.

# *Epilogue*

They waited until April for the wedding. It took that long to handle all the paperwork associated with Russ's inheritance, to set up the trusts and for Sydney to pay off all her father's debts.

Lowell appeared to be doing a lot better. He'd joined a grief-management group and had started working again. Sydney had patiently showed him how to keep the books—something he'd never bothered with when Shirley was around to handle it.

"I'll get the hang of it," he'd said as he struggled with learning the accounting computer program. "I appreciate everything you've done, Sydney, but you have your own life to lead."

"I'll always be just a phone call away," she said, and she'd said it again and again as she'd made all the arrangements to move her things down to Texas.

But finally it was all done. Sydney had taken out a Yellow Pages ad, and Russ had helped her set up a spare bedroom in his house as her home office.

By April 1st, she was officially a Texan and about to officially become a married woman. She'd never had a single qualm about marrying Russ. The fact he was stubborn about some things—like his absolute refusal to be interviewed by any reporter—only made him more appealing.

They'd intentionally kept the wedding low-key. Although the press had lost interest in Russ soon after reporting that he was giving his money away, Sydney didn't want to take any chances. So they had the wedding at Russ's home and invited only family and a few close friends. Sydney had worn her mother's 1970s wedding dress, which was simple and classic and had made Lowell cry, but in a good way. The ceremony was short and sweet, and afterward, in true Texas style, they had a barbecue.

Sydney, literally wearing a trash bag over her dress, sat at a picnic table making a dent in a plate of ribs. Russ was in the backyard playing with a couple of kids—Bert's great-grandkids—and Blossom. He'd already changed out of his dress clothes, which didn't surprise her. He might look great in a well-tailored suit, but he was far more comfortable in his jeans.

"He's gonna be great when y'all have kids of your own," Lowell said. He was sitting beside Sydney at the picnic table, chowing down on a chicken leg. "And this'll be a great place to raise 'em. Man, it's beautiful here. I haven't been back in so long, I'd forgotten how beautiful spring in Texas could be."

Sometimes Sydney forgot her dad had been raised here. "Who would have ever guessed that I'd be moving to a small town in Texas?"

"Well, it's in your blood, I guess. You have a lot of your mother in you, but you have a lot of me, too."

Sydney considered that a high compliment. "Thanks, Dad."

"What would you think about having me as a neighbor?"

"What?" Had she heard right?

"There's a nice little lake house just down the road that's for sale. It needs work, but that's okay."

"What about Baines & Baines?"

He sighed. "Fact is, the work's no fun without your mother. Thanks to you, I'm fixed to retire early and I'm thinking that's what I'd like to do. Get away from those cold New York winters. Do some fishing—I used to win prizes in bass tournaments. I bet you didn't know that."

No, she didn't. "Oh, Dad, I'd love to have you down here. Aunt Carol would love it, too. And if you get bored you could do some work for me."

"I'll do it, then."

Russ joined them at the picnic table. He had a grass stain on his shoulder and a piece of grass in his hair, which Sydney lovingly removed. Her handsome husband. She had to pinch herself hourly, because she was so happy it almost had to be a dream. And now her father would be close by.

Her whole family. Russ didn't yet know, but there would be another family member come next November. She smiled a secret smile, anticipating the look on his face when she told him. They'd been reasonably careful about birth control... though there was that one time. That was all it took, apparently. Her future son or daughter was just as stubborn and determined as his or her father.

And that wasn't necessarily a bad thing.

# Harlequin® Historical
### Historical Romantic Adventure!

# A WESTERN WINTER WONDERLAND

## with three fantastic stories
## by
## Cheryl St.John,
## Jenna Kernan
## and Pam Crooks

Don't miss these three
unforgettable stories about
the struggles of the Wild West
and the strong women who
find love and happiness
on Christmas Day.

Look for
A WESTERN WINTER
WONDERLAND

*Available October
wherever you buy books.*

Ria Sterling has the gift—or is it a curse?—
of seeing a person's future in his or her
photograph. Unfortunately, when detective
Carrick Jones brings her a missing person's
case, she glimpses his partner's ID—and
sees imminent murder. And when her vision
comes true, Ria becomes the prime suspect.
Carrick isn't convinced this beautiful woman
committed the crime...but does he believe
she has the special powers to solve it?

Look for

# Seeing Is Believing

by

# Kate Austin

Available October
wherever you buy books.

HN88144

Silhouette
Desire

There was only one man for the job—
an impossible-to-resist maverick
she knew she didn't dare fall for.

# MAVERICK
## (#1827)

BY *NEW YORK TIMES*
BESTSELLING AUTHOR
## JOAN HOHL

### "Will You Do It for One Million Dollars?"

Any other time, Tanner Wolfe would have balked at being
hired by a woman. Yet Brianna Stewart was desperate to
engage the infamous bounty hunter. The price was just
high enough to gain Tanner's interest…Brianna's beauty
definitely strong enough to keep it. But he wasn't about
to allow her to tag along on his mission. He worked
alone. Always had. Always would. However, he'd never
confronted a more determined client than Brianna. She
wasn't taking no for an answer—not about anything.

Perhaps a million-dollar bounty was not the only thing
this maverick was about to gain….

## Look for MAVERICK

*Available October 2007 wherever you buy books.*

# REQUEST YOUR FREE BOOKS!
## 2 FREE NOVELS PLUS 2
# FREE GIFTS!

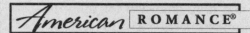

## Heart, Home & Happiness!

HAR07

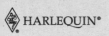

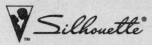

## Romantic
# SUSPENSE

### Sparked by Danger,
### Fueled by Passion.

When evidence is found that Mallory Dawes
intends to sell the personal financial information
of government employees to "the Russian,"
OMEGA engages undercover agent Cutter Smith.
Tailing her all the way to France, Cutter is
fighting a growing attraction to Mallory while at
the same time having to determine her connection
to "the Russian." Is Mallory really the mouse in
this game of cat and mouse?

## Look for

# *Stranded with a Spy*

## by *USA TODAY* bestselling author

# Merline Lovelace

### *October 2007.*

Also available October wherever you buy books:

BULLETPROOF MARRIAGE *(Mission: Impassioned)*
by Karen Whiddon

A HERO'S REDEMPTION *(Haven)* by Suzanne McMinn

TOUCHED BY FIRE by Elizabeth Sinclair

# HARLEQUIN®

# *Mediterranean* NIGHTS™

Sail aboard the luxurious Alexandra's Dream *and*
experience glamour, romance, mystery *and* revenge!

**Coming in October 2007...**

# AN AFFAIR TO REMEMBER

*by*

## Karen Kendall

When Captain Nikolas Pappas first fell in love with
Helena Stamos, he was a penniless deckhand and she
was the daughter of a shipping magnate. But he's
never forgiven himself for the way he left her—and
fifteen years later, he's determined to win her back.

Though the attraction is still there, Helena is hesitant
to get involved. Nick left her once...what's to stop
him from doing it again?

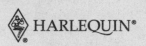

# HARLEQUIN®

## American ROMANCE®

# COMING NEXT MONTH

**#1181 THE RANCHER'S FAMILY THANKSGIVING**
**by Cathy Gillen Thacker**
*Texas Legacies: The Carrigans*
Susie Carrigan and Tyler McCabe have always been friends—and sometimes
lovers. Both fiercely independent, they've never been a couple, and never sought
marriage. To anyone. But once Susie's matchmaking parents start setting her up
on dates, Tyler starts thinking about their "friendship" differently. And wants
those other guys to stay away from "his girl"!

**#1182 MARRIAGE ON HER MIND by Cindi Myers**
With a failed wedding behind her, Casey Jernigan arrives in eccentric Crested
Butte, Colorado, ready for single life. But her landlord, Max Overbridge, could
challenge that decision. His easygoing charm and his obvious interest are making
her reconsider those wedding bells!

**#1183 THE GOOD MOTHER by Shelley Galloway**
*Motherhood*
Evie Ray and August Meyer were once high-school sweethearts. Now Evie's a
single mom, doing her best to juggle work and motherhood, while August has
taken over his parents' vacation resort. Seeing each other again, they realize
there are still sparks between them. But will they be able to overcome past hurts
to find love again?

**#1184 FOR THE CHILDREN by Marin Thomas**
*Hearts of Appalachia*
Self-reliant schoolteacher Jo Macpherson is on a mission to instill pride in the
children of a Scotch-Irish clan living in Heather's Hollow, in Appalachia. She
never expected to have to deal with intrepid Sullivan Mooreland, a far too
appealing newspaperman who's on a mission to track down information about
the Hollow that Jo has vowed not to reveal.

www.eHarlequin.com

HARCNM0907